FREE TO GOOD HOME

FREE TO GOOD HOME

COLLECTED SHORT STORIES

Anne Kelleher

ISBN-13: 9780692408186
ISBN-10: 0692408185
Library of Congress Control Number: 2015940138
Pond House Press, Canton, CT

TABLE OF CONTENTS

FREE TO GOOD HOME

———

The first time Marvin thinks about adoption is at Passover, when his mother burns the gefilte fish. The second is a few weeks later, when she leaves the group from the casino bus, and is found stuffing dollar bills into g-strings at a strip club. And the third is the following morning, when she refuses to even discuss the possibility of giving up the third-floor walk-up she shared with Marvin's father, and moving in with Marvin and his family.

But as usual, it's his wife who brings it up. She has a pamphlet from the Family Adoption Unit of the Community Center, and she pushes it toward him as the dino-bot removes their plates. Deb doesn't say anything as she slides the glossy pamphlet across the table.

He glances down as the dino-bot places a plate with a slice of lemon merengue pie in front of him. The pamphlet reads: "WHEN IT'S TIME TO SEVER THE CORD" and features a photograph of a smiling gray-haired woman embraced by a younger couple and children, as another younger couple drives off waving in the background.

"You can't be serious," says Marvin, as he plunges his fork into the pie.

"Of course, I'm serious," replies Deb. "Look at how happy Ruth's family is with the grandparents they picked up. Look at how happy the kids are. Why should we deny your mother the same chance for happiness?"

Marvin stares across the table at his wife of seventeen, nearly eighteen years. His mother has been a widow for three years; he expects her to be unhappy. She was devoted to his father; unhappiness should be her natural state.

"Of course she's unhappy," he says when he can, the sticky sweet citrus taste clinging to his tongue. "She's getting old, her mind's going, she's lost my dad. I expect her to be unhappy. Don't you?" One of Deb's prize Abyssinians whines around his ankles and he automatically reaches down to stroke the soft spot between its ears.

Deb hesitates, cocks her head. She pushes the button on the table panel that summons the dino-bot. When it appears, she puts the plate with the pie on its serving surface. "I think it's a bit stale," she says.

"NO-TED," answers the robotic voice. It swings around, its pincers poised to remove Marvin's plate but he grabs it out of the thing's mechanized reach just in time.

"Hold on there, cowboy," he says. "It tastes just fine to me."

Defeated, the arm retreats. Marvin watches the dino-bot disappear into the kitchen, then looks at Deb. "You can't be serious."

"I think we should go talk to them, Marvin," Deb replies. She picks up her coffee cup, takes a sip and sets it down. "Especially if you think your mother's mind is going. I don't know I'm really equipped to handle that." She gently removes a kitten from the table and stares at him until he opens the pamphlet.

When the phone rings in the middle of the night, Marvin doesn't think he's really equipped to handle it either, especially when it turns out that the person on the other end is his mother. At the police station.

"She's been arrested," he explains to Deb as he climbs into his street clothes. "Someone has to go bail her out."

"I'm not kidding, Marvin," says Deb, as she rolls over and goes back to sleep. "If your mother is going through some strange old-age thing… I'm just not prepared."

At the station, Marvin is shown into a little room that's painted gray on the bottom and blue on top. There's a battered table and three folding chairs. "Have a seat," says his uniformed escort. "Your mother was picked up for soliciting, but since it seems to have been a misunderstanding, we're letting her go. This time."

"Soliciting?" Marvin stares up at the woman's impassive face. "Soliciting as in prostitution? Are you kidding? My mother's... my mother's old enough to be a grandmother."

"Old enough to be a great-grandmother," says a familiar voice from the open doorway, behind the bulk of the watch officer.

The neighborhood watch officer stares down at Marvin. Disgust flickers across her expressionless face. "Not sex. Pot. Pot brownies, to be specific."

"They're banana muffins, I told you," says Marvin's mother from the hallway.

Contempt vies with disgust as the officer stands aside to allow his mother to enter the room. "Just wait here, ma'am. With your son. We're almost finished the processing."

"What processing?" asks Marvin, as his mother sits down in the metal chair opposite Marvin.

"Paperwork, you know," the officer shrugs as she turns to leave. "I'll be back in a few. Bathrooms are that way. Water's down there."

"Isn't everything digitized?" Marvin asks. "I thought... I thought the government went paperless last year?" It was a huge project, an enormous advance in the history of mankind, according to the news.

"Of course it's all digitized," says the officer. "But we still call it that."

Left alone, as the officer's footsteps fade down the hall, Marvin looks at his mother. She's wearing a flowered housecoat and slippers. Her hair resembles a dandelion going to seed. "Mother," he says. "What's wrong with you? You look like a crazy person. Are you feeling all right? Have you been taking your medicine?"

"Nothing's wrong with me," she bristles. "This is what I was wearing when they picked me up. Don't you think I asked them if I could change?"

Marvin rolls his eyes and shakes his head. He never knew his grandmother, and the woman in front of him is turning into a stranger. "I can't believe you got yourself arrested, Mom... what were you thinking? Or not thinking, because obviously you weren't."

"I was trying to help someone," she answers quietly, so quietly he almost can't hear her.

Marvin shakes his head again. "I just don't know why you won't move in with us, Mom. We'd love to have you, me and Deb. We're your family, don't you want to be with us?"

"You and Deb and her forty nine prize Abyssinians? No, thank you. I've already told you – a thousand times. I'm not moving in with a woman who'd rather raise cats than kids."

In that moment, the officer walks back into a room, carrying an electronic note pad. "Here you go, Mrs. Simkus. Just sign here."

His mother signs her name with a flourish. Backwards. The notescreen refuses to take it.

"What the fuck, Mom?" Marvin explodes out of his chair. "What the fuck is wrong with you?"

"Did you know only ten percent of people can write backwards at all," says his mother, resigning her name in the right direction. "It's how Leonardo kept his notebooks. They can all be read perfectly if you hold them up to a mirror. Did you know that?"

Marvin glances at the officer, who's looking at him with what can only be sympathy. "Whatever, Mom. It's after 3 AM. Can we go home, please?"

In the car on the way home, his mother places a tentative hand on Marvin's arm which he impatiently shakes off. "I'm awfully sorry to make you come get me, Marvin. But my choice was either call you or spend the night in the cell."

He looks at her sideways as she continues, "And you wouldn't want that for your mother, would you?"

He takes a deep breath as he slows to a red light. Deb would have a field day with that question. What, after all, really was it he wanted for a mother? He was silent the rest of the way, thinking it over. Maybe adoption really was the answer, for both of them, for all of them.

After all, wouldn't it be nice to have a mother who wasn't allergic to cats? A mother who didn't wake him up in the middle of the night asking to be bailed out? A mother who didn't try to share her marginally legal medicine in the most illegal of ways?

He could hear all those questions in Deb's voice.

When he pulls up to the curb, his mother looks at him before she opens the door. "You have to come up with me," she says.

He groans.

"I don't have my purse." She spreads her hands apart. "I can get into the hallway, but I can't get into my apartment without my card."

Her palm print opens the front door. He trails her up the steps. On the second floor landing, the paintings start, wide swaths of neon colors that wildly cut across the dingy background in swirling rainbows. "Who did this?" Even under the dimmed-down night-lights, the colors hurt his eyes.

"Me," says his mother, with a sniff. "No one's painted those walls in fifteen years." She pauses on the third floor landing, turns and looks down, at the stupefied expression on his upturned face. "Marvin, stop looking at me like I've grown two heads. No one gives a fucking shit."

There's no reason to feel ashamed or upset about those feelings," says Ms. Wagner, the beautifully-coiffed woman behind the desk at the Community Center. She leans across her desk. "In the old days, people didn't realize that it's okay to acknowledge that just because someone gave birth to us, it doesn't mean you're a good long-term fit."

"I don't want her to feel abandoned," says Marvin. The wad of paper towels he stuck under his arms in the men's room, just before coming into the room, is slipping under one arm and feeling wet and clumpy under the other.

"Of course not," says Ms. Wagner. "And she won't be... until her application is approved, accepted and she's adopted... she's still your mother. In every sense of the word." She pauses, looks back and forth between the two of them. "Maybe you'd like to take our DVD home, Mr. Simkus. It might help you... make up your mind." She smiles, a little gently, a little sadly. "You know...adoption works best when all parties involved find a congruent fit. We encourage you to look at our list of avail-"

"I don't know I'm ready to replace my mother-in-law," says Deb. "Even with someone who loves cats."

"You might not be, not yet," replies Ms. Wagner. "But keep an open mind and open heart. Adoption goes both ways."

With that, she stands up and shakes their hands.

In the parking lot, Marvin hands Deb the DVD. "Why don't you watch this?"

"She's your mother, Marvin," Deb replies, pushing it back into his hand. "I think you should go watch it with her." She reaches up, and gives him a kiss on his cheek. "I have to get back to work. I'll see you after dinner. Make sure that dino-bot got rid of that awful pie. It's been hanging around the kitchen for more than a week."

She turns on her heel and strides away to the auto-strip, leaving him standing beside his mini-ped staring after her.

He finds his mother in the galley kitchen, coloring in the flowers on the black and white modernist-print wallpaper his father had painstakingly installed a couple years before he died.

For a few minutes, Marvin stands in the doorway, watching in near-disbelief as she works away, wearing one of his father's once pristine white shirts, whistling under her breath.

He decides a calm approach is best. She is, after all, the woman who gave him life, the one who raised him, the person who'd more or less done all she could to make sure he'd turned out as normal as possible. Which he had, which is why he knows for sure, watching his mother switch from glitter markers to water-color pens, she's gone around the bend. "Hello, Mother."

She looks up immediately. "Hello, darling. Try not to talk to me like we're in a black and white movie, okay?"

He raises his eyebrows. So this was how it was going to be. "Are you sure you wouldn't like a kitten, Mother?"

"Are you trying to turn me into a crazy cat lady, Marvin?"

He smiles, just a little, to make sure she understands he realizes she's made a joke. "I-I just thought...Deb and I just thought something to take care of might be good for you... now that you're rattling around this place all alone."

She puts the caps back on the markers and turns to face him. "This place is the size of a shoebox. I couldn't rattle in here if I tried. And God knows, I have." She pushes past him, heading toward the bathroom.

"What do you mean by that, Mother? What on earth are you talking about?" He asks, as she closes the door in his face.

"You're getting yourself too upset, Marvin," she says when she comes out. "It's not good for you."

"I agree it's not good for me," he says, following her back to the kitchen. "But you're the one who's upsetting. I hardly know this person you're turning into, Mother.... Getting yourself arrested, going to strip clubs, painting on walls. What are things coming to, Mother, what are you thinking?"

By the time he's finished, she's standing still, beside her markers. "I'm thinking like me, Marvin."

He takes another deep breath, then reaches into his pocket and pulls out the DVD. He places it on the kitchen table. "Deb and I... well, we were thinking that maybe... maybe you'd be open to considering this. Not that... not that I want you to feel we're kicking you out, you understand. Or abandoning you. We just...we just think you'd be happier... well, we just think you'd be happier with someone else."

It's cowardly, he knows it, as he taps the DVD, then turns on his heel, and flees. He runs down the steps, out the door, and throws the car into gear as fast as he can turn the key.

A few days later, Marvin is surprised to hear not from his mother, but from Ms. Wagner at the Community Center. "Mr. Simkus?" she says, as soon as he says hello. "I'm thrilled, absolutely thrilled. We just love it when a family comes together."

"What?" Marvin manages at last. "What are you talking about?"

"Your mother's adoption – or rather, should I say, your former mother's adoption? So smooth, so easy. Worked out well for everyone involved, I think?"

"You mean... you mean, my mother's already someone else's mother?"

"Mothers are at a premium," says Ms. Wagner. "And a bona fide Jewish mother...let me tell you, the only other more sought after is an Italian mother, but it takes a special family to keep one long term. Jewish mothers, on the other hand...a single placement is usually all it takes."

"Goodness," says Marvin faintly.

Deb comes into the room, a basket full of bloody towels in her arms. "I have good news, great news and bad news," she says. "The good news is Mrs. Snitz had her kittens. The great news is they're all healthy. The bad news is she had them in your sock drawer."

Marvin holds up his hand to forestall Deb, and frowns as he tries to concentrate. "So, so... you're really telling me... that's it? That's all there is to it?"

"There's a couple forms for you to sign, of course... your mother – I mean, your former mother – has already taken care of all of hers. I'm sending your documents over now... check your e-mail. They should be there by the time we're finished."

"Already?" Marvin just can't believe it's all happening so fast. "I...I just... who are these people? Who...where... how did it all happen so fast?"

"Mr. Simkus," Ms. Wagner says gently. "A lovely couple with a new baby girl, if you must know - although all parties involved have requested anonymity, at least initially. Your former mother had all this in motion for months."

About a year later, Marvin is standing in line at the bakery department of his favorite grocery store when he hears a familiar voice say his name. He turns around to see his mother – his former mother – smiling over a grocery cart, in which sits an adorably chubby toddler of some indeterminate age. From the pink bow in the child's hair, he guesses it's a girl. The bow matches the one in his mother's – his former mother's.

"Hi," he answers, faintly, wondering how to address her. "Mom" is no longer applicable, "Shirley" feels too presumptuous. And he has no idea what her last name is now.

"Meet my granddaughter, Rudy Patootie," Marvin's former mother says, eyes shining. "My boys are around here somewhere –"

"Your boys? You have grandsons, too?"

"Oh, no, I meant Dave and Bernie. Dave and Bernie, my new boys... though really it's Bernie who's my boy. They're around here somewhere – I left Bernie in the cheese department and Davie's in the baby aisle." She turns to go, smiling brightly. "You look good, Marvin. Glad to see you looking so well."

"Wait," he says, even though he hears his number called. "The lady at the agency... she told me... you'd had the adoption all in motion... weeks before I brought it up?"

With a glance over her shoulder and a caress of the child's ringletted head, Marvin's former mother pushes the cart a bit closer. "It's for the best, don't you think? Marvin, really. Once your dad died, wasn't it obvious? You're not the son I needed; I'm not the mother you want."

"Shirley?"

Marvin looks up as a man's voice intrudes. The man coming toward them is waving a bouquet of multi-colored roses in one hand and a package of diapers in the other. The child bounces and waves her hands.

Automatically Marvin steps back.

Shirley touches Marvin's cheek in the briefest of caresses, as she swings the grocery cart in the direction of the flower-bearing stranger. "We're so lucky it's not the old days," she says. "When people thought the only way to make a family was with blood."

The End

AFTER THE RAPTURE

———

Bess's first inkling that the financial markets really had predicted the end of the world came when she awoke before 4 AM on April Fool's Day to check the futures. It took her a few minutes to ease herself out of Kitty's embrace, because the warm nest of her wife's body was almost too inviting to leave.

But the niggling sense of unease, the one she'd gone to bed with, the one that had been growing stronger over the last few days, that something was about to happen... something big and bad and akin to aliens' landing...wouldn't let her keep her eyes closed.

For the past week, and for no apparent reason that neither she, the firm's market analysts, nor all the Talking Heads both online and on TV were able to discern, the broad market indicators had been going nuts. Crazy nuts, as in far beyond the normal tides of chaos that periodically upended Wall Street.

Stocks of all kinds started freefalling for no apparent reason – and then reversed themselves just as suddenly; some clients called, demanding to know when she was going to buy more of everything, while others – in full panic mode – demanded she abandon all positions and convert directly to cash. Or gold... except for the fact that gold was the one thing that appeared to have a clear and obvious direction: straight down.

It took her about twenty minutes of clicking through every television station before she thought about waking Kitty. It could all mean nothing, Bess told herself, as she stood in the middle of the windowed aerie that served as her home office, surrounded by the pine branches and the scent of the Kona coffee that was beginning to permeate the entire house.

I should just go back to bed, she told herself as she glanced out the window above her desk. It was still too dark to see anything outside. The sun wouldn't be up for another hour or so at least. That's what she should do... crawl back beneath the covers, snuggle up to Kitty's generous curves. After all, in their little slice of paradise, deep in the Connecticut woods, the cable went out from time to time.

The problem was that the cable *wasn't* out. The problem was that every channel in the world seemed to be broadcasting the rainbow bars of the emergency broadcasting station, and the conversation – the near argument - she'd had at the end of the day with Doug Rambowski which was unpleasantly looping round her mind as the persistent bars on the TV.

A devout Christian, Doug was convinced the "last days" were close at hand... and equally convinced that "the gays" as he'd say with a glance at Bess...were about to be "left behind." Doug was also convinced that the anomalies in the markets meant that the "last day" was literally about to be "any day" and lately, he'd had no compunction about sharing his views, even when no one was listening.

Normally, Bess dismissed his nonsense. Surely this morning was just a coincidence, just a problem with the cable company, not a sign from God. Bess didn't have time for arguing about which God was the right God, when the only God she'd ever heard about growing up hated her. She attended the Unitarian Church with Kitty and everyone there seemed to believe there could be a much nicer version of God – if any – than she did. Which was lovely, and Bess was always happy to support whatever Worthy Cause the church was supporting every week, if only to make Kitty happy. Because, after all, she'd walk on glass to make Kitty happy. She put the remote down and decided Kitty was probably happier staying asleep.

I'm being ridiculous, Bess told herself, as she made her way to the kitchen they'd redone a few years ago, to Kitty's specifications, with one of Bess's much-maligned Wall Street bonuses. Together, they'd created a culinary dream space, with marble counters and custom Shaker-style cabinets, Danish appliances and enormous windows that, at this hour, offered a view of the lights of Hartford twinkling like fairy dust in the distance.

At least, they usually offered a view of the lights of Hartford. Bess put her mug down on the counter and opened the French doors that led to the three-season sun room. It was still chilly this early in the spring; they hadn't used it yet this year. The room with its curving bay windows, and doors leading to the deck, offered the best view of the valley, especially now, while the trees were still bare. The cold air slapped her face, and made her wince as it hit her bare ankles, but at least she was sure she wasn't dreaming.

Bess grabbed the binoculars. She trained the lenses on the sky. Stars twinkled back, pinpricks of light in the velvety black. Sunrise was at least an hour or more away. The city's lights should still be visible. Where was Hartford? Was it possible there was some kind of regional blackout?

At least their lights were still on.

But for how long, who knew?

With a deep sense of foreboding, Bess tiptoed back through the silent hallways, to the bedroom she shared with Kitty. For a second, she hesitated, wondering if she was being silly. Since when had she allowed anything Doug Rambowski, or anyone who believed anything even remotely similar to what Doug professed, to affect her in any way at all... except maybe amusement?

I should just get back in bed until the sun comes up, she thought, hesitating by the bed. It's a regional blackout, there's a problem with the cable company. Everything will be back to normal in a few hours. I'll go to work, the futures will be up, gold will be plummeting, and all the lights will be on everywhere.

It is, after all, April Fool's Day.

"What's wrong, babe?" Kitty's soft voice made Bess jump. In the dark, she felt Kitty fumble for her hand. "I'm sorry, didn't you think I was awake? Is everything okay?"

"I don't know." Bess drew a deep breath. "Maybe I'm just going over the deep end. Maybe I've finally let Doug Rambowski get to me. Maybe it's time I quit the business."

Kitty sat up, tugging at Bess's hand. "Honey, what's wrong?"

Bess hesitated. But the die, after all, was already cast. Kitty was awake. "Well… for one thing, every TV station in the world seems to have gone off the air, and for another… Hartford seems to have disappeared."

"What? What do you mean… Hartford's disappeared? You mean like… Brigadoon?"

Bess sighed. "Come on. I'll show you."

Kitty swung her legs over the edge of the bed as Bess handed her a robe. "Show me what?"

"Every channel's…off. And the lights of Hartford… have gone completely dark."

"Not that there were that many lights to begin with," muttered Kitty as she followed Bess down the hall, her old ballet slippers making no sound at all on the bare wood floors. In the kitchen, she paused in front of the coffee machine and gestured to the little television mounted over the wine fridge. "Show me."

For a split second, Bess wanted to tell her to go back to the warm cotton nest, to dismiss her own intuition that in the night, something – maybe everything – had changed. She loved Kitty so much, her instinct to protect so strong, it was on the tip of her tongue to try and make a joke of it. Instead she flicked on the TV. The screen flickered to life, but the only image that filled it was a rainbow of lifeless bars, with a ticker running beneath it that read, in alternating English and Spanish, *PLEASE STAND BY…*

"Watch." Bess clicked through the stations. On every station, both image and message were the same, except on stations like Al Jazeera, where the message was in Arabic and English.

"Okay," said Kitty. She moved a bit closer, and put her arm around Bess's waist, nestled her arm around Bess's waist. "But so what?"

"Look outside."

With a questioning expression, Kitty crossed the wide floor and peered out the window, into the darkness. Beyond the tree line, the palest edge of dawn limned the rounded edges of the far hills. But otherwise, even from where Bess stood, she could see it was completely dark.

"At this hour, there should be lights," said Bess, quietly. "The airport… the planes… look, Kitty…look how dark."

Kitty turned to face Bess. "A power outage, don't you think?"

"And we still have power?" Bess looked from the wine fridge to the stainless steel behemoth Kitty picked out to chill everything else. "How does a tiny little town like Wincanton all the way out here in the woods have power and Hartford not?"

Kitty took a deep breath. "Well…" She walked back to the mugs and poured two cups of coffee. "Isn't that what we voted for, a year ago last November? That's what I voted for." She cast a quick glance over her shoulder at Bess and winked. "I'm not sure what you voted for."

"What are you talking about?"

"The back-up power grid, off the old hydro-electric plant on the river… you remember? The referendum? Whether the town should tap into it, even though it was going to cost a gazillion dollars to make all the conversions and connections and transformations?" Kitty offered a mug to Bess, then took a sip of steaming coffee. "Mm. Oh, yes, I'm so glad that passed." When she saw Bess wasn't drinking, she put her mug down on the counter. "Babe. Talk to me. What has you so spooked?"

"I don't know," Bess shrugged. She usually dealt in dollars and cents and had to be reminded sometimes that wallets came attached to human beings. She wrapped her arms around Kitty, pulled her close and nestled her head into the sweet coarse terrycloth of Kitty's shoulder. "Just a feeling, I guess…ever since yesterday… and… that idiot, Doug Rambowski."

For a brief moment, Kitty lingered in the embrace, then drew away. The image on the television screen painted her face with a ghostly rainbow. "Honey, have you checked the radio? The internet?"

Bess shook her head. "Not yet. I saw this… and…." She shook her head, closed her eyes. "Things haven't just been *bad* in the markets the last few days, Kitty…things have been *strange*, things have been weird. Stocks are tanking one minute, then skyrocketing the next, oil and gold and the futures in general are sinking into historic lows, clients are freaking out… and did you know the Great Lakes and the Mississippi have all turned red? Blood red?"

Kitty cocked her head. "There's an algae bloom… they say it's caused by the warm winter…I think I mentioned it the other day and you didn't seem to take notice."

Bess shrugged. "Well, I guess I did. You know I only pretend to be the tough one."

"Come on." Kitty gently removed the remote, and replaced it with her own soft palm. "Drink your coffee. Then get your work laptop, and let's get online. If something's really happened, your firm will surely let everyone know about it first."

Bess bounded up the steps to her office, retrieved her laptop, and returned, to find Kitty clicking through the channels on the kitchen TV.

"Finding anything," Bess asked, as she plugged in her laptop on the breakfast bar.

"No," answered Kitty. "What I don't understand is, if there's an emergency, why hasn't the emergency network started broadcasting? Isn't that what it's supposed to do? Maybe we should try the radio? We have one somewhere, right?"

"We have one through the TV, sweetie," said Bess. "Let me just try a few things here…." She broke off and shook her head as she fruitlessly clicked through blank screen after blank screen. Whatever happened, seemed to have happened on or around midnight. "Because what I don't understand is why I can get onto the Internet, but the company's intranet – our internal site - doesn't seem to exist?"

Kitty came to stand behind her, placed a mug next to the keyboard. "Well," she said, very softly, almost directly into Bess's ear, "you know it *is* April Fool's Day. Right?"

Of course it was some kind of joke. A really awful joke, and whoever perpetrated it was in incredible trouble; that had to be the explanation. Even the radio yielded nothing but static.

There was nothing to do but go back to bed. That is, until they noticed a pair of headlights creeping their cautious way down the long gravel drive.

The motion sensors snapped on the floodlights as the car approached the house, to reveal a battered red Subaru. Kitty squinted as the driver got out of the car. "That's Will Olmstead," she said. "The library guy... the one on the board of the CSA?"

"The guy whose picture is next to the word "crunchy" in the dictionary? Oh, yeah." Bess rolled her eyes.

"I'll go see what's up," Kitty said.

"Not without me, you don't. It's not even 6 AM." Bess followed as the doorbell chimed.

"Good morning, Will." Kitty swung the heavy oak door wide, wide enough for Bess to see that Will's car held other people – a young woman in the front seat, and maybe two or three school-aged kids in the back. "Everything okay?"

The look on Will's grizzled face was pure relief, which surprised Bess, but what really surprised her was when he leaped forward and enfolded both women in a bear hug. "Thank God. Thank God... I saw your lights back here from the road, and so we decided to take a chance. Do you know every other house on this street so far is empty?"

"Empty?" echoed Kitty. "What do you mean... empty?"

"Everyone's gone," Will answered.

For a long moment the weight of his words lingered in the still air, added to the look Bess exchanged with Kitty.

"What are you talking about," Bess demanded. "What do you mean…everyone's gone?"

"Their stuff is all there – cars, jewelry, clothes, TV's," Will continued. "Their pets are still there… dogs, cats, birds, guinea pigs… you name it. But the people… so far you're the first house on this whole street with a human soul in it, let alone two."

"Where did everyone go?" asked Kitty.

"Beats the shit out of me, pardon my French. I got a call from my daughter… about midnight. Her son of a bitch husband passed out on the couch about eight last night. When she got up to check on him around one, he was gone."

"So?" asked Bess. Something about all this was suddenly making her really angry. Who was this old coot to just show up at the crack of dawn, scaring the hell out of Kitty? "You said he's a son of a bitch… so he got up in the middle of the night and left her. What's so strange about that?" SOB's have been leaving women since the dawn of time. It was one reason she thanked the Universe every day for making her a gold-star lesbian.

"Nothing, except for the fact he left every stitch of clothing, in the exact shape as when he was wearing it. And his watch, and his wallet and his keys, and his truck." Will took a deep breath, let out a long sigh. "Oh, and his cellphone. I wouldn't believe it if I hadn't seen it for myself. I got to get Caroline and the kids back to my place – they're all a little freaked out." He turned on the stoop as if to go, then paused. "I was thinking maybe we could all get together… later. Maybe around noon, one o'clock? I'll get the word out on the library web site…the Internet seems to be the only thing working." He glanced from Kitty to Bess, then back. "Have you tried your phones? Mine doesn't seem to be working any more. Neither's Caroline's."

"You said your daughter called you around one?"

"That was the last call I got… the last call she made." He shrugged, then shoved his hands deep into the pockets of his denim jacket. "So we'll say noon, at the library?"

"Sure," replied Kitty, in the silence, because Bess suddenly couldn't bring herself to speak. "We'll be there, won't we, Bess?"

In true Kitty-cat fashion, Kitty decided to make muffins to take to the town meeting while Bess combed the Internet for any kind of news. Whatever happened, happened around midnight, no matter where. On the New York Times site, she found the final headline: Four Horsemen of the Apocalypse? Beneath were photographs of the alleged heads of the latest terrorist groups. Bess found herself skimming the entire article, which talked about the most recent credible threats. Jesus, Bess breathed, was it possible that this was what had precipitated the real apocalypse?

She clicked through more sites, growing more and more alarmed by what she read. Doug Rambowski wasn't the only one who thought the end of the world was at hand. So, apparently, did everyone else, from the Dalai Lama, who acknowledged he may not have a successor, to the scientists talking global gloom and doom at the latest environmental summit.

"Maybe it could be possible," Bess said, more to herself than to Kitty, who placed a steaming muffin dripping butter on a plate beside the computer.

"Anything's possible, right?" Kitty held up the coffee pot. "Freshen up?"

"Is that really all you can think about," Bess asked. "Muffins? Coffee?"

"What else should I be thinking about?" replied Kitty.

"If this really is the Rapture, the end times, that Doug's been talking about, don't you see we're fucked? So what if most everyone is gone... according to everything I'm reading here, the one's who're left are screwed – big time."

For a long moment, Kitty gazed steadily into Bess's eyes. "It's true we don't know what's going to happen, Bessie. But in the meantime, until we do, the coffee's hot and the muffins're warm. Don't you think we ought to enjoy?"

Bess hesitated, gazing back at her wife, uncertain of what to say. Visions of every dystopic future ever proposed by movie or novel danced through her mind, from drug-crazed motorcycle gangs out to "purge" the land to brown shirts goose-stepping down Main Street. *Mad Max. A Clockwork Orange. The Road. The Walking Dead.*

Nothing felt safe, let alone cozy. Nothing good ever happened after the end of civilization. She was beginning to think they should be getting dressed and going to town, to try and grab some supplies to stockpile, before the invaders – whoever they might be – arrived and tried to take it all away from them. She really didn't think it was time to enjoy hot coffee and fresh muffins.

Bess opened her mouth to answer, but a short, sharp bark at the back door interrupted her. "What the hell?"

"Sounds like one of those dogs Will was talking about," Kitty said. She put the coffee pot on the counter and went to peer out the door. "Aw..." Before Bess could stop her, she had the door unlocked.

"Kitty!"

Kitty paused, with her hand on the knob. "Bessie? What's wrong? It's a little Yorkie out there... at least I think it's a Yorkie... it could be a Maltese."

"Don't you dare open that door...it could be a trap."

"A trap?" Kitty stared. "Are you serious?" She looked out the window again. "It's just a little dog, Bess...wearing a leash. It's got to be a pet...someone's pet. Don't be silly."

"If you open the door, make it quick."

"Oh, my heaven." Kitty rolled her eyes, but did as Bess asked. She pulled open the door, grabbed the dog, and brought it inside. The tiny animal whimpered and wagged its tail frantically, leaping in her arms to try and cover her face with kisses.

"What about the floors?" asked Bess, as Kitty headed toward the kitchen, crooning.

"What?" Kitty turned in mid-step, the dog cradled to her breasts. "You think the world's come to some sort of end, and you're worried about our floors?" She didn't wait for an answer. She simply turned on her heel, talking to the dog.

Bess sank onto her stool at the breakfast bar, watching Kitty. The muffin still dripped butter, the coffee still steamed. She took a few sips of coffee, watching Kitty, then took the pot back to the machine.

Kitty was bending over the dog, as it wolfed down sliced chicken from last night's dinner. That is, if anything that looked like a slipper covered in fur could be said to "wolf" down anything.

Bess touched her shoulder. "I'm sorry."

Swiftly, Kitty placed her hand over Bess's. "It's okay. Maybe we'll find his owner."

Bess took a deep breath. "Maybe." But she knew that they both doubted it.

Kitty bathed it ... him... in the laundry room sink and used her blow dryer to make him fluffy. He leapt onto the couch and divided his time between watching Bess and following Kitty every time she moved out of eyesight.

"Maybe he has a chip," said Kitty. "He had a collar."

"And a leash," said Bess, trying not to sound hopeful.

He was definitely coming when they bundled themselves and the muffins into Bess's Jeep. He made it to Kitty's seat in two swift leaps. She laughed, and cradled him on her lap. Bess shook her head and put the car in gear.

Neither of them spoke as Bess drove down through the empty streets. The stark spring sun shone through the skeletal branches, a few of last year's rusty leaves clung to gray branches. Bess wondered if they were the only ones left in town... them and Crunchy Will.

"Maybe we're the only ones left," said Kitty, cradling the dog.

"You're reading my mind again." Bess tried a smile, but she wasn't sure Kitty bought it.

"I don't want you to think I'm not scared, too," said Kitty.

They rolled to a stop at the red light at the first large intersection. Bess looked right, then left, then right, up and down.   No other cars were on the road. "Fuck it," she said.

She lifted her foot off the brake and was about to hit the accelerator when Kitty cried, "Wait!" She pointed across the street. "Look. Those ladies... on the corner. See them? Over there?"

Ladies was a word to be used loosely, thought Bess, as she eased the car through the intersection, and pulled up beside the three people on the corner. They looked lost, alone and very afraid, although a kind of wary hope crossed the face of the youngest. She looked to be about sixteen, and in her arms, she clutched an infant. "You ladies okay?" Bess asked, cracking the window just a touch.

Kitty jostled her elbow. "Put it down more."

"What if they have a gun?" Bess mouthed back.

Kitty's eyes flew open. No words were necessary. Bess turned back to the window. "You all okay?" she repeated.

They glanced at each other before the teenager answered. "We don't know, ma'am. To tell you the truth... we're not sure where we are. We left Hartford as soon as the sun came up... started walking toward the lights we saw out this way. But we haven't seen anyone on the way... you're the first ones."

Kitty jostled Bess's elbow again. "Let them in."

"What?" Bess startled. "Are you kidding?"

"We can't leave them here, Bess." Kitty had never sounded so sure of anything in her life.

Bess shook her head. She'd been counting on the space in the back of the Jeep for supplies. But surely at the town meeting there'd be someone who'd know what to do with these refugees. That's what they smelled like, as they piled into the back seat of the Jeep, the children making small little squeaks. But otherwise, the adults were almost too quiet, even though they responded to Kitty's questions with tight smiles and little nods.

The smell – a cross between old cheese and a latrine - nearly nauseated Bess.

Once they crossed the first intersection, there appeared to be more signs of people. They passed a couple walking three dogs, who waved at them as enthusiastically as if they were long lost friends. And as they approached the green, Bess could see at least three dozen or so vehicles of all shapes and sizes parked neatly around the perimeter.

Their approach was heralded with all the pomp as if they were visiting royalty. As she helped the old lady from the car, she heard a young boy shout, "We got at least six more coming!"

As the group tumbled out of the car, Bess counted the three adults, the infant, and four children who had to range in age from maybe two to six or seven. Had there really been that many when they'd gotten into the car? Maybe I am dreaming, she thought, as she slowly followed them up the sidewalk to town hall.

"Kitty! Bess!"

She heard their names as soon as they entered Town Hall. A couple she recognized from church rushed up to them, and then another few, as they made their way across the vestibule. Kitty was immediately enmeshed in conversation. Bess paused on the periphery, taking it all in.

In the main meeting space, about half the seats were already occupied. About thirty or forty more milled around the room, some with clipboards. Bess recognized a few of the faces, from gay rights' meetings, from non-profit boards and a couple from local government.

"Kitty, we're so glad to see you both," said one woman with a clipboard, who came up to greet the group. "Bess, you probably don't remember me... I'm Aina...we had a plot next to yours at the community garden last summer? Our paths didn't cross much but Kitty talked about you so much I feel we're old friends." She held out her hand.

Bess shook it, still trying to get her bearings to pay attention to the questions Aina was asking the others. A kind of order was being established, as adults clustered toward the stage, with a few of the older teens gathering up the younger kids and heading toward the playground on the other side of the building. A group of young men and women were bringing in boxes of supplies, like diapers and bottles of water.

Crunchy Will and about half a dozen others dressed in equal amounts of denim and flannel were on the stage, playing with laptops, jotting notes, conferring in low voices.

"Come on," said Kitty, tugging on Beth's elbow. "Let's go find seats."

As Bess followed Kitty down the center aisle, she saw two men come through the side door. Unlike any of the other men present, both were wearing blazers, ties and crisp-looking shirts. They were clean-shaven, in their 30's. Backlit by the bright spring day, all their other features shadowed, they looked like big black birds against the sun.

"Here," said Kitty, pulling Bess into a seat on the side aisle.

Bess turned to see where the two men had gone, when Crunchy Will walked to the edge of the stage.

"Good morning, everyone... or I guess it's afternoon by this time. Happy April Fool's Day... but believe me, as far as we can tell... what's happened is no joke."

"What has happened?" shouted someone from the other side of the room. "What the fuck is going on? Where's the police?"

Will held up his hands. "I know you're upset. We're all upset, believe me... we've all lost... we've all lost... just about everyone. Family members, friends, neighbors, co-workers... people are just... gone."

"Where the hell did they go?" This time, Bess recognized the woman who spoke from the front of the room.

Will smiled down at her. "Amy, we don't know. From what we've been able to figure out so far... about two-thirds of the town have... vanished. And from what we're able to put together from the Internet ... there are folks in other places... and the ratio seems about the same. So far. But this is all... preliminary. We don't... we don't really know much yet."

"And you're not afraid whoever took them won't be back for the rest of us?"

Will glanced at the people on the stage. "We have no way of knowing that... because we don't know yet what happened. And I say... yet... because we will figure it out. Sooner or later."

"It's the Rapture, Will," shouted someone else. "Don't you realize... this is the Rapture. And we're the ones who are left."

A nervous ripple of what sounded like it could be laughter went through the crowd, like a cold wind over a field of wheat. Bess glanced around the room. At least she wasn't the only one. A few more people were actually shrugging shoulders and nodding heads.

"What if that's true?" Another woman, this one just a few seats away from Kitty, spoke up. "We're laughing, but what if it's true? If we're the ones who're left, aren't we screwed?"

The group on the stage looked at each other nervously and Bess felt cold all over. Of course they were screwed. Everyone knew that if the end of the world happened, it was going to be bad.

"I'm not sure," answered Will. "The one thing I can promise you is that we have plenty of food. We have plenty of everything, as a matter of fact. We may not know how to access it, and we may fumble a time or two getting things back to as close to normal as we can make them. But, for example, I know that as long as the river keeps flowing, we'll have enough power to keep the lights on in Wincanton. We have the technology to figure out how to turn the lights on in Hartford, too. So until we get things running again, which I have no doubt we will... we just have to keep from panicking. We have to try not to be afraid, and not to let our fears about what could happen interfere with the reality of what is happening. We don't have to turn on each other, because, really, there's nothing to fight over. We have lots... and lots... of everything."

For now, thought Bess, envisioning a myriad of possibilities, each worse than the last. But just about everyone else around her seemed to be smiling and nodding.

Someone from deep in the crowd on the other side of the room shouted, "What about the police? Any signs of them?"

A lone man approached the edge of the stage. "So far... I'm the only one left in three towns."

Great, thought Bess. *Just great.* They were peaches ripe for the plucking.

Kitty raised her hand, stood up when Will recognized her. "Maybe we don't need police." She gestured around the room, to the back, where the distribution of supplies continued quietly. "We seem to be doing okay so far." A ripple of laughter went around the room. "And from who I see here so far... none of us look very dangerous – I mean, I know most of you. The last thing we need to worry about are police."

"What are you afraid of, sir?" asked Will.

As the speaker enumerated a litany of concerns, most of which Bess shared, she was startled by a voice in her ear.

"You look like someone who understands why we need police."

She turned to see one of the two men from the doorway smiling at her from the row directly behind her and Kitty. For some reason she found that disquieting. "I guess I appreciate law and order... doesn't everyone?"

"Do they?" replied the man in the tie. His shirt was very white, very starched. He smelled vaguely like Bess's suits when they came back from the drycleaner. "Do these people here? Doesn't sound like it to me." He shrugged, then nodded to the stage, wearing an expression that wasn't quite a smile.

Troubled, Bess turned around, listening as more and more of those present seemed to agree with Kitty and Crunchy Will that there were far more important things to worry about than the police. As a proposal to establish a police force got tabled – for the moment, Crunchy Will made sure to say several times – Bess watched as everyone agreed about everything. There was no rancor, no bitterness, no shouting.

What the hell was going on?

"Maybe they put something in the water already," said the same voice.

Bess jumped, startled. She glanced over her shoulder. The man smiled back, imperturbably. "That's crazy..." she began, but he interrupted her.

"You ever see a public meeting where everyone agreed?" He leaned forward, touched her shoulder, and spoke almost directly into her ear. "Think about it."

Too stunned by the breadth of the conspiracy he implied to answer immediately, Beth drew a deep breath, staring at him in dismay. His mouth stretched wider, but it still wasn't really a smile. It was an imitation of a smile, a realization that made her even colder.

Kitty touched her shoulder. "Bessie, you okay?"

"Oh," Bess turned around with relief. "Yeah. Sorry. Got distracted for a minute."

"You don't mind, right?"

"I don't mind what?"

"Bringing home one of these refugee families… like the ones we picked up? Just until we figure out what's what?"

"What are you talking about?" Bess stared at Kitty. Somehow in the last few minutes, the meeting had broken up. People were standing and hugging. Crunchy Will was telling everyone to keep checking the library website. He'd be posting all the information they had as soon as they had it.

Aina came up, armed with her clipboard and a grin that stretched from ear to ear. "We knew we could count on you folks. I understand you have a street full of empty houses… if you would let us use your house as a relocation center – temporarily, of course."

"A what?" interrupted Bess. "A relocation center? Kitty, are you kidding?" She looked at Aina. "Would you please excuse us?" When Aina had turned away with a nod and a troubled expression, Bess hissed at Kitty, "What have you signed us up for?"

"There aren't that many people left," Kitty answered. "And those of us who are… we have to help each other."

"That means we have to let them in our house? It's one thing to bring in a dog, Kitty, but whole families? Strangers? From God only knows where? Are you kidding?"

"It wouldn't be very long…there's lots of empty houses."

"Then maybe they should go there…what about bedbugs and the smell and the food…"

"There's lots of food," said Kitty. "We have showers. We can find them new clothes."

Suddenly Bess was aware of the man in the row behind her, the man with the tie. He was sitting very still, obviously listening to every word.

Bess looked at Kitty, at the kindness in her eyes, the softness in her expression. But she wasn't smiling, and she didn't look happy. What did it matter how clean the house was… if Kitty wasn't happy? What did bedbugs matter, in the face of Kitty's reproach?

"We can share," said Kitty. "Don't you think?"

For a long moment, Bess hesitated. She could feel the man behind them, leaning into their argument, into Kitty's distress. No, she thought. That's not going to happen. The days of just writing checks for Kitty's causes were over. Whatever had happened, she understood that more would be asked of her. And for Kitty…she'd walk on glass. "Okay."

As she spoke the word, the side door swung open, and a shaft of sunlight sliced through the auditorium. It fell directly on the man with the tie, and Bess blinked.

When she opened her eyes, he was gone. Except for his blazer, his shirt, his trousers, his shoes. And his tie.

"Okay," Bess repeated.

She was silent on the way home. She knew Kitty watched her, but she wasn't sure what to say. Maybe the man in the tie had just… left. Nude? In a crowd of maybe sixty or seventy people? Not likely.

But if he hadn't… where'd he gone?

"Are you upset, Bessie?" asked Kitty, when they turned down the drive. "We don't have to take anyone in… we don't have to do anything you're not comfortable doing. I know this is probably going to affect you a lot more than it will me."

"Why?" asked Bess, puzzled.

"Because, well, for one thing… I know almost everyone in town who's still here. How many do you know?"

Bess stared at the road ahead, thinking furiously. By sight... maybe half. She had the feeling she was going to know all of them, very well, very soon. "I guess you have a point, sweetie. And no, I'm not upset. You can bring home anyone you want - dogs, cats, guinea pigs... no rats, though, okay? I can't do rats."

"Are you sure? How about single mothers, or homeless teens?"

"Those, too." Bess reached for Kitty's hand and squeezed it. "Anyone. As long as it makes you happy."

"Can I ask you something?" asked Kitty when they pulled up to the house.

"Do you really have to ask me that?" asked Bess.

"You looked like you were talking to someone as one point, Bessie."

"I was," Bess answered as she unlocked the front door for the last time. "Didn't you see him? The guy in the tie?"

"No," said Kitty. "I saw some clothes on the chair... but I didn't see him. What did he say to you?"

"He thought I looked like someone who understood why we need police," replied Bess. She held out her arms, enfolded Kitty in a hard embrace.

"And are you, my beloved?" laughed Kitty from the hollow of Bess's neck.

"No," said Bess. "Or if I ever was... not anymore."

The End

ENHANCED

The rows of smiling children's faces on the revolving screens on the walls stared back at Rachel while the numbers on the clock on the coffee table clicked inexorably toward 12. The doctor went to lunch at 12.

Rich was late, as usual, but to be fair, his job and his office were on the other side of the city. Maybe there was a traffic backup somewhere. Rachel telecommuted to her job as a data entry analyst; as long as the data got entered on time, it was easier for her to leave her desk whenever she wanted or needed.

The receptionist at the console cleared her throat. "If your spouse doesn't arrive in the next five minutes, I'm afraid we'll have to reschedule. Dr. Jorgenson goes to lunch –"

"At twelve," Rachel said. "I'll see if he's called." She rummaged through her bag, searching for the PCD which she knew had to be stuck somewhere between all the detritus the mother of a seven year old accumulated. A small container of Sam's favorite hard candies tumbled out of the bag, onto her lap and under her chair, followed by the ball of yarn and knitting needles she'd just purchased to make Rich a sweater for his birthday, and finally her lipstick.

She grabbed for the yarn, for the candy box, and her lipstick, which rolled under her chair. Beneath the receptionist's disapproving eye, Rachel peered under the seat, and saw what looked like curled scraps of paper on the carpet. She picked up one, smoothed it flat. It was a white oval, with the word MAYDAY printed in black block letters. In addition to the ones on the carpet, there were a bunch more stuck to the underside of her seat. A little kid had had a field day.

She gathered her own belongings, then picked up the stickers off the carpet, and rolled them into a ball. She approached the receptionist. "Is there a trash can? I... I picked these up under the chairs over there. Some... some little kid must've stuck them underneath the seats." She held up the wadded up ball of stickers, in reparation for Rich's tardiness.

The receptionist gasped. Her cheeks flushed an ugly red, and she looked from the stickers, then back to Rachel, eyes narrowing. "You.... where did these... how did ....did you put them there?" she stammered.

Rachel blinked. "You've been sitting here watching me since I arrived. Did you see me on my hands and knees putting stickers under chairs?"

In that very moment, the door to the hallway slid open, and Rich bounded over the threshold. "Sorry, sorry, babe," he muttered. "Not too late, am I?" He glanced up at the receptionist with his trademark charming grin and a flash of his blue-green eyes with the gold-brown flecks, that matched the yarn Rachel had so painstakingly picked out. "The traffic getting over this way was nuts."

"Not yet," the receptionist replied with an audible sniff and a disapproving glance. She took the stickers from Rachel's fingers with an expression bordering on disgust, then touched the screen on the desk before her. She looked up and said, "The doctor will see you now."

Rachel was surprised when they were ushered into an office that, except for the diplomas displayed proudly on the one wall that wasn't a complete sheet of glass, bore more resemblance to the office of an attorney-at-law than a doctor of medicine.

Nevertheless, the doctor who strode in just after they were seated, was wearing a set of full medical scrubs under his long white coat, and he somehow gave the impression he had either stepped out of the operating room or was about to step into one. "I understand we're here to discuss your son, Sam?"

Rachel nodded and Rich leaned forward. "You bet." He picked up Rachel's hand and squeezed it, looking as excited as a kid about to be admitted to the circus. Or a freak show. "We're interested in a full enhancement."

"Really," Dr. Jorgenson said. "You know a full enhancement now includes vision. And by the time your son's through the approval process, hearing as well."

"How... how does a baseball player's performance improve with better hearing?" asked Rachel.

There was a short silence and the doctor looked at her, finally making eye contact. "Mrs. Ingot. You have a lot of questions. We all do, actually. Let me start by asking you one... tell me about Sam?"

"Sam's seven," she began.

"And wants to be a ball player," interrupted Rich. "More than anything."

Dr. Jorgenson smiled. "Both great places to start, Mr. and Mrs. Ingot. A perfect age to begin the enhancement process, and a perfect aspiration. So, let's talk a little more. Health history?"

"I haven't missed a day since I started at CyberBi," answered Rich. "And Rachel... well, except for when she had Sam... you're a healthy one, too, right, sweetheart?"

"I think Dr. Jorgenson means Sam," Rachel says carefully. "He's been a normal kid. A few colds, the flu last year, nothing serious."

"No broken bones, no issues with joints, ligaments, that sort of thing?"

"Never," they say together.

"Height and weight? Your boy, I mean, not you." Dr. Jorgenson's teeth practically sparkled as he winked.

"At his last check up, I think he was about forty-eight inches and he weighed maybe sixty pounds?"

The doctor entered the information into a screen embedded on his desk. "Healthy boy. I see we already have his records. Excellent. So... what are your questions for me?"

"That's it?" Rachel asked.

"I'm sorry," Dr. Jorgenson said. "Was there something else you want me to know about Sam?"

Rich looked at Rachel. Rachel looked at Rich. "Well... don't you want to know... anything else?"

"Mrs. Ingot," said Dr. Jorgenson. "If Sam's accepted into the program, we're going to get to know each other incredibly well. So considering we only have another ten minutes together...what can I tell you?"

"How much does it hurt?" blurted Rachel.

"How long's it take," asked Rich at the same time.

Dr. Jorgenson held up his hands with another sparkly smile. "One at a time, folks. But to your point, Mom, we have wonderful pain management methods. Most kids report almost no discomfort after the first month or so post-ops."

"Post-ops?"

"It's not possible to perform the full enhancement procedures in one operation," said the doctor. "At least not on kids, not yet. Our instruments are good, but not that good, not yet. We do the lower extremities, the shoulders and the elbows. Then we give it time to heal and about six months later, we do the eyes, and soon, of course, the ears."

"What do you do to the eyes and the ears?" asked Rachel, feeling faintly nauseous, thinking of Sam's big blue eyes, so like his daddy's.

"We provide full 360 degree day and night vision, as well as the ability to see movement of up to 350 milliseconds. Using a highly calibrated implant, we can increase hearing to up to ... well, about the level of your average bloodhound's. And what parent wouldn't want that? No more pretending not to hear you." He laughed again, and slapped the desk surface. "No more pretending at all."

"I guess I don't understand why a ball player needs to have such sensitive hearing," said Rachel.

"Are you kidding, honey?" said Rich. "You'd know what the other team was saying, the coaches, the players... you'd know what your own team was saying, from across the field. Of course, enhanced hearing would be useful." He grinned at Dr. Jorgenson.

"You betcha," said the doctor. "I'm sure you've seen and heard about some of our success stories." He leaned over, rummaged in a desk drawer and removed a portable viewing device so compact it was no thicker than a sheet of old-fashioned paper. "I'll tell you what. I know you have a lot of questions, and I know we're all very busy people. Why don't you take this with you? It's got all our most frequently asked questions, patient and parent interviews, and most importantly, exclusive footage with Connor Wazilusky and Euell Grantham."

"The Wazz, himself?" said Rich. "Really?"

"The one who started it all," replied Dr. Jorgenson.

"What about doctors? The places all this gets done?" asked Rachel. She watched the silver screen spring to life under Rich's gleeful taps.

"Those are there, too, Mrs. Ingot," said Dr. Jorgenson. He got to his feet, and looked at his watch. "If you decide to go forward with the process, call my admin. It was good to meet you both." Without waiting for a reply, he strode toward the door.

"W-wait," said Rich. "What about this?" He held up the PVD.

"Keep it as long as it takes you to make a decision," answered the doctor.

"And if we have more questions?" asked Rachel, as the door clicked closed behind the doctor's back.

"Wow," said Rich. "We must look like we can't afford it."

"But our insurance would cover –"

He reached over, jiggled her knee. "Just an expression, Rach."

On the wall behind the desk, a cuckoo clock began to sing.

At least Rich agreed not to allow Sam to know the PVD existed until both of them had had a chance to go through its entire contents. Which, as far as Rachel was concerned could take a year. Maybe two.

Of course if Rich had his way, they'd be viewing it as a family instead of Saturday morning cartoons. Which was tomorrow.

She caught Rich sneaking a peek at it when she returned to their table from the ladies' room that evening during their weekly date night dinner. "Sweetie," she said, in a stage whisper, "You know they can ask us to hand over our PVD's until we leave, right?"

Immediately, Rich tapped the screen closed, and looked up with a guilty expression. "I can't help it, Rach. I just want to see what they say about the Wazz. You know he was my hero growing up. I wanted to be a ball player just like him, you know that."

Rach took a deep breath, cocked her head and chose her words with care. "I thought your dad was your hero."

Rich had the grace to look sheepish. He tucked the device into his pocket and picked up his silverware. "Of course my dad's my hero. But he left baseball, to go to war, and came home and had me and Rob. The Wazz left baseball, went to war, came home and made history." He shrugged and cut into his cauliflower cheese.

Rachel sipped her wine. The Wazz had made history, all right. He was the first athlete in the history of the world to turn a step on a land-mine into something to be celebrated. Suddenly the hundreds of thousands of men and women who'd survived the war on terror but lived with artificial limbs weren't seen as people with disabilities.

Suddenly everyone realized they had *enhanced* abilities. Somewhere along the line, technology began to, if not outstrip biology, at least, as Rich liked to say, give it a run for its money. And slowly and surely technology did, as more and more enhanced athletes took to fields, courts and stadiums far and wide.

It took about a dozen years before someone had the bright idea to enhance young athletes. Emerging athletes, the euphemism went. Children, as Rachel thought of them. Little children, some young as five.

When a distant cousin of Rich's manager at CyberBiologics was accepted into the program a couple years ago, right around the time they signed Sam up for T-ball, the idea occurred to Rich.

And like a dog with a bone, he wouldn't let it go.

"You're not even going to keep an open mind about all this, are you, Rachel?"

Lost in her thoughts, Rachel hadn't noticed she had finished her wine, and Rich his cauliflower cheese. "Rich, stop. Not here, okay? Of course, I'm going to keep an open mind. I understand the...opportunities this opens up for Sam."

"I know you look at him and see your little boy. But you have to look past that, Rach. You have to look past the big blue eyes and the soft blond curls. You blink and he's going to be a man." He leaned forward. "This is our chance to make him Superman."

Rachel took a deep breath. But what if he doesn't want to be Superman? She wanted to scream, but didn't, because to do that would be to engage a battle she wasn't prepared to fight. What was wrong with Sam growing into the man Sam was born to be? Instead she smiled up at the waiter. "I will definitely have another glass of wine."

They managed to talk about other things for the rest of the evening, but as they were pulling up to the house, Rich put a hand on Rachel's knee. "Just promise you'll keep an open mind?"

"Always," she managed.

Once inside, Rich paid the sitter and Rachel went to check on a sleeping Sam. Curled up on his side, one hand tucked around his tiger and the other under his cheek, he looked no older four or five. She straightened and tucked the tangled covers around the curves of his legs, the angle of his feet. Then she bent and kissed the top of his curly head. For a moment she paused, breathing in the salty sweetness of his little-boy smell.

She rose, slowly, gazing down. Rich was all for the enhancement, there was no doubt about that. If he'd had his way, Sam would be halfway through the process by now. But what about Sam, she wondered. Of course he'd be swayed by talk of baseball and ball games, the roar of the crowds, the crack of the bats. What little boy wouldn't be, especially when it was something his daddy he adored wanted so badly? She was afraid Sam was going to be all too easy for Rich to convince. But how, she wondered, how on earth was he going to convince her to agree to cut off those little-boy legs?

The next morning – Saturday – Rachel left Rich and Sam eating pancakes and watching the cartoons while she went off to yoga class, stayed for the optional meditation, and joined the group for coffee afterwards. Or, in her case, almond milk chai latte.

"We're thinking of having Sam enhanced," she replied, to Ceci's query about what was new. She glanced around, uncertain as to her announcement's reception. "You know baseball was always Rich's dream," she said. She pulled her knitting needles out of her bag and began to knit. If she wanted to get this sweater done by his birthday in November, she had to make the most of every opportunity when she wasn't working and Rich wasn't around.

"Wow," said Beryl, at the far end of the booth. "Did you hear about that kid from Sunbury who just got picked up by the Yankee organization? I hear he signed for over 100 million a year....and he's not even eleven."

"Dollars?" asked Anita, always the skeptical one. "Dollars or credos?"

"Who cares?" put in Ceci. "Dollars or credos, that's a shit load of money. And last year... or maybe it was just a few months ago, there was that kid from Hartford who got a football contract down in Dallas. He bought his mother a tropical island for Christmas. Or maybe it was a house on a tropical island."

"Did you hear the NBA's negotiating with the players' union to raise the baskets again?"

"Didn't they just raise them at the beginning of last season?"

"Yes," replied Beryl. "But the new round of enhanced prospects are so superior to the previous rounds... twenty –five feet is a piece of cake." She looked at Rachel. "So, wow, you're going to go for it, huh?"

Rachel hesitated. "We're considering it. We went to the Jorgenson Clinic yesterday... we have information. Rich is all for it, of course, but... well... I guess I'm not so sure."

"It's clear Sam has ability, Rachel," said Anita. Her son, Josh, had played on every team with Sam since T-ball. "And didn't Rich almost make it to the majors?"

"I suppose he might've made it if he'd been enhanced," Rachel said. "He... he got caught in the cross-hairs, he likes to say. When Rich was coming up, enhanced players were becoming the next great thing. No one wanted a guy who was going to wear out at thirty-five, or forty."

"Ah," said Ceci. "That's sad. No wonder he wants Sam enhanced. He wants his son to have the shot he never had."

"But you're not sure," asked Beryl. She licked the chocolate from her fingers.

"It's a pretty drastic process," answered Rachel. "They don't do the procedures all at once like they do with adults... with kids it has to be done over a couple years. So the kid loses a lot of school time... and I'm worried that Sam is at such a critical stage right now... he gets behind now he might never catch up."

"He gets a professional contract, he won't have to," laughed Beryl.

"No one will be able to catch up to him," put in Ceci.

"Hey," said a woman, tapping Rachel on the shoulder as she went by her chair on the way to the ladies' room. "I think you dropped this?"

Rachel paused the rapid click of her needles and glanced back. The woman was holding out a white card. The word MAYDAY was printed on it in black block letters, just like the stickers at Dr. Jorgenson's office. "No," she said, glancing up and shaking her head. "No, not me." She smiled, turned back and started knitting again.

"You'll be set for life, Rachel, if you do this," said Beryl. "Will you remember us when you do?"

"How could I forget any of you?" Rachel smiled at each one in turn. "But...what I keep wondering is... what if Sam doesn't get a contract? If something goes wrong....then what?"

It was a question no one knew the answer to, because no one could think of anyone who'd had a child enhanced who didn't get a contract with some professional organization or another. Enhanced athletes – or EA's – were simply too valuable not to hire.

But still, thought Rachel, on the drive home. Nothing worked one hundred per cent of the time. Medical procedures went wrong, even the most mundane and routine carried risks. So how likely was it that there would be some sort of complication? Hopefully, that information would all be contained in the FAQ's.

And hopefully, Rich would've finished with the PVD so she'd have a chance to look at it. And look at it. And look at it.

Because, after all, they'd agreed they wouldn't even bring up the subject to Sam until they'd both reviewed the information.

Sam greeted her at the door with an enthusiastic, "Mom, I'm going to be as great as the Wazz was!"

Startled, Rachel halted, just over the threshold. From the doorway, she could see all the way into the family room, where Rich was curled on the couch, holding the silver PVD, wearing a sheepish grin. She took a deep breath, mentally counted to ten. "Sweetie," she says. "I saw Hunter out riding his bike. Why don't you go play, too?"

When Sam was safely halfway down the street, she shut the front door.

"I know you're pissed," said Rich, as she was hanging up her jacket.

"I'm concerned," Rachel replied. "This is a big decision... the biggest decision we'll ever make for him. I just want to get it right."

"Rach, I know that, I agree with that."

"And you also agreed we wouldn't talk about it with Sam until we both had a chance to look through the material." She didn't wait for an answer. She walked into the kitchen and punched her favorite coffee code into the machine above the counter.

He followed, like a puppy, waving the PVD. "Well, come on... Sam's outside... we're not busy...let's look at it."

Rachel took a deep breath. "Well... as a matter of fact, I am busy. I have to stuff to do now...chores, and such. It's Saturday afternoon, remember?"

"You know, Rach, I thought we were going to look at this together... this morning before Sam got up. I wasn't expecting you to book out on me."

"I always go to yoga."

"And you just said this was the biggest decision we could ever make for Sam. Don't you think you could've missed yoga just this once?"

The coffee finished brewing with a shriek that echoed the one in Rachel's head. She picked up the cup, and turned around with a determined smile fixed on her lips. "Okay. Let's look now."

The opening montage alone brought unwilling tears to her eyes, so admittedly inspiring was the journey of a man who returned from war refusing to believe himself broken, and in the process, transforming himself into a global hero and the entire sports world.

But the rest of the presentation... or as much of it as they were able to watch before Sam came back inside and the PVD went into her desk drawer... her locked desk drawer... raised as many questions as it answered.

It wasn't until Monday morning – after Sam went to school and Rich went to work and before her weekly conference call – that Rachel had time to really study some of the Frequently Asked Questions. But none of them seemed to be about complications. Nothing in the entire presentation suggested anything but that nothing but billion dollar contracts ever came of enhancement.

There was something else that troubled her. Sam wouldn't just give up two years of his life...they'd have to give up two years of theirs. And move... to the one of the "clinic locations" which were hinted at, but not specified. They all involved a lot of beach and sun, wherever they were. No wonder Rich was so enthused.

It all looked so easy, so glossy, so glowing. All they had to do was hand over their little boy.

Stop it, she told herself. That's hardly keeping the open mind she'd promised Rich. She glanced at the clock, torn between starting at the beginning and writing down her questions, or taking a few minutes to clear her head before her call.

She opted to clear her head.

At the end of the street, on the far side of the cul-de-sac, was a little park that had been built in commemoration of the family who'd died in the house that had once stood there. When Sam was a baby, she used to walk him there. The sound of the fountain in the reflecting pool soothed them both. With all the neighbors either at work or telecommuting, at this hour of the day, she was almost sure to be alone.

She put her shoes on, grabbed a jacket and her knitting bag. The morning air was chilly. She trudged down the quiet street. A few front doors were open, a few cars were in the driveways. She could hear music blaring from the upper windows of one house: Tabby Jamison was home sick. Again.

She reached the little park, followed the yellow brick path to the center, where the fountain splashed a cheery gurgle. As she suspected, she was completely alone. She sank onto the white bench, and stared into the bubbling pool. Copper pennies glinted at the bottom – the neighborhood kids had turned the fountain into a wishing well a long time ago.

I should make a wish, too, she thought. But what should I wish for? That Sam get a billion dollar contract? That Rich drop this whole idea? She stared up at the sky, at the trees, at the tulips that were just beginning to open in fat clumps around the fountain. But nothing answered.

I should go home, Rachel thought. Review my notes, get ready for the call. She had work to do, real work, the kind of work that paid the bills. Whatever decision they were going to make, they weren't going to make it today.

"Sassy, come back here!" The voice intruded before the dog, a black lab at the end of a long purple leash came bounding up the path. She stopped when she saw Rachel, gave a short bark that sounded more like a greeting than a threat and ran up wagging her tail.

Sassy the black lab was the neighborhood escape artist. Rachel knew her owners, Les and Barbara, only by sight. They were an older couple, had moved into the neighborhood when the houses were new. Their children were raised and grown, and Sassy the lab, as far as Rachel could tell, was now the lucky beneficiary of their cumulative years of taking care of everyone.

Sassy plunked herself down at Rachel's feet and proceeded to stare into Rachel's eyes with her big brown dog eyes. "Sorry, puppy," said Rachel. "I don't have any treats."

"Oh, she doesn't need any treats, believe me." Barbara, sixtyish and stylish, stepped around the corner. "I'm sorry, I hope she's not disturbing you... Rachel, right? You live in the Harrison house. I'm Barbara Hower... you and your little boy have brought Sassy home a time or two."

"Yes," Rachel answered. "She must be doing better, though... I haven't seen her lately."

Barbara sat on the bench beside Rachel, and picked up Sassy's leash. "We were away for a while." Barbara looked into the fountain, a crease between her eyes. She turned back to Rachel with a smile that didn't quite reach her eyes. "But we're back now and happy to be here." Before Rachel could say anything else, Barbara continued, "I hear you're having your son enhanced."

Rachel looked at her, shocked. Yes, she'd mentioned it to her yoga friends, but how on earth had this woman – this stranger – heard?

"Your son told me," Barbara said, gently, as if she could read Rachel's mind. "He's excited."

"We haven't made any decisions yet," said Rachel, too shocked almost, to speak. How could Rich not have realized that Sam wouldn't be able to stay quiet until a decision had been reached? Sassy put a paw on Rachel's knee and whined, and she automatically stroked the dog's head. What had he been thinking? Sam was probably telling the entire school yard at that very moment.

"I'm glad to hear that," replied Barbara, after a little silence. "It's not something to be undertaken lightly."

Rachel gazed at the woman. She was staring into the fountain, the dog's leash twined around her fingers. "Do you... do you know anyone who... who's been enhanced? Or... their child?"

Barbara took a deep breath, her eyes fixed on the water. "A few years ago, there was a family who... who decided to do it. The Tysons. They left maybe a year or so before you moved in."

Rachel shifted in her seat, her heart beginning to pound. "Do you know... uh... have you kept in touch with them? I'd love to talk to another parent...someone who's been through the process...they say in the PVD you can't talk to people until the initial clearances have been obtained."

"Hm," Barbara said. "There's a group... you might want to talk to. Before you make any decisions."

"A group?"

"A group," replied Barbara. "Of mostly parents... moms, dads, grandparents. A few pediatricians. But..." She reached into her pocked and removed a small white card, about half the size of a normal business card. She handed it to Rachel.

The one side was blank. The other side said MAYDAY in black block letters.

"Mayday," breathed Rachel. "I saw this in the doctor's office, and then, the other day in the café.... What the hell does Mayday mean?"

"In French, it means 'help me.'" Answered Barbara. "Originally it was MAEDAE... until someone realized the correlation to mayday – as in m'aidez?"

"I don't understand," said Rachel. "M-A-E, M-A-Y, what does it stand for?"

"Moms against enhancement, Dads against enhancement," replied Barbara. "Here's what you do. Go to the Paradise Café over on

Morningside Ave. Order whatever you want, and hand this to the clerk under the top bill when you pay. And make sure you pay in dollars, even though they'll offer to let you pay in credos. He'll take it from there."

"What?" Rachel stared from the small piece of cardboard to Barbara. "What do you mean, he'll take it from there?"

"He'll tell you how to get the information you want."

"Why can't you?"

Barbara gazed steadily at Rachel. "Because I don't have it. I can only point you in the direction you said you wanted to go."

Rachel looked down at the card, turning it over in her hands like the thoughts tumbling in her head. "I…I don't understand. Are you trying to tell me that there's something about the enhancement process that… that no one wants us to know?"

Barbara sighed. She shifted on the seat, took a deep breath, then glanced around the small enclosure. "You thought 1984 was just a novel, didn't you?"

More confused than ever, Rachel cocked her head. "What? 1984? What does some old book have to do with… enhancement?"

"Nothing," answered Barbara with a sigh. "Nothing… and everything." She got up, touched Rachel's shoulder. "Keep asking questions. Just realize… there're some answers you're not going to want to know."

Morningside Avenue was on the other side of town, the sketchy side of town. Which wasn't a place Rachel ever frequented. She parked her car in the parking lot between the café and the laundromat next door. She glanced up and down the street, then made sure to lock the doors.

The café reminded her of the places she used to frequent in college, fair trade coffee, organic desserts, and lots of local art. The scent of cinnamon enfolded her the moment she opened the door. She stepped over the threshold and headed for the counter. The girl behind the counter didn't look much older than Sam, but she smiled brightly when Rachel stepped up. "Help you, miss?"

The pastries in the case made her mouth water. Rachel pointed to the organic chocolate chip cookies, the cinnamon shortbreads. Just the thing for dessert. "Three chocolate chip, three of those cinnamon ones?"

"They just came out of the oven," the girl smiled. "Don't they smell great?"

The air of unreality swirled around Rachel's head. I'm not supposed to be here, she thought. I'm supposed to be home, calculating whatever it is I'm supposed to be calculating today. I'm a mother, a wife, a responsible employee. I'm not a... she glanced around the shop. Whatever or whoever it is who comes here.

"Thirty-nine credos," the girl said from behind the register. She paused, looked at Rachel up and down. "Or dollars. Whichever you prefer."

Rachel reached into her purse, carefully counted out the dollars, and then placed the small MAYDAY card under the top dollar so that the edge of the card just peeked over, just as Barbara had explained to do. The girl took the wad of cash, then painstakingly began to count. "One...two... oh," she muttered, when she saw the MayDay card. "Sure... um....Hang on a second." She counted out the rest of the cash, and shut the register. Then she reached under the counter and pulled out a clipboard.

An old-fashioned pencil was attached to the top by a string. Across the top, Rachel read "Employment Application."

"This way," the girl said.

She pushed through a beaded curtain. Rachel followed. The girl gestured to a curtained alcove, which turned out to contain a battered wooden desk and chair. "You can sit here," she said.

"But...but," said Rachel. "I...I'm not looking for a job."

The girl looked at her with what could only be pity. "I know that." She tapped the chair back. "Under the application... you'll find what you're looking for there."

"I don't understand," said Rachel, sinking into the seat. "What's going on? Why all the secrecy?"

"Just read," replied the girl. "And you will."

She was gone before Rachel could ask anything more. The scent of patchouli and cinnamon drifted from the curtain, the air inside was hot. The walls were painted a dingy mustard. The chair squeaked every time she shifted.

She turned the employment application over. Open the drawer was all it said.

In the drawer was a small track-viewer, the kind that couldn't be connected to the Internet, the kind used in classrooms and by parents like Rachel and Rich to entertain their kids without fear. And the kind used by criminals because their activities couldn't be traced.

Rachel placed the device on the desk, took a deep breath and, pressing her forefinger squarely onto the keypad, turned it on. The keypad turned green, highlighting the ghostly image of her fingerprint. The screen flickered and leaped to life.

A pleasant looking woman's face filled the screen. "Hello," she said. "If you are viewing this, I hope it is because you wish to save another child from the horror of enhancement. What you are about to see will shock you, horrify you, and might even sicken you. What are you about to see is the truth."

Fifteen minutes was enough for Rachel. She burst into the café, where the only patrons were the desultory man drowsing in the corner, and a couple women who appeared to be studying. She found the girl behind the counter in the kitchen, bringing out a tray of cookies. For a moment she wanted to knock the hot tray out of the girl's hands. How can anyone bake cookies when this is going on, she wanted to scream. But she didn't. Instead she said, "I want to talk to someone."

"Okay," the girl answered. She placed the hot tray on a cooling rack, picked up one that had been cooling.

"How?" demanded Rachel, following her. "How do I do that?" She held out the viewer. "None of this… none of this can possibly be true."

The girl slammed the tray down on the glass case. The other patrons looked up and the girl grabbed the device. "I know you're upset. Give that to me." She pushed the viewer into the front pocket of her apron.

"Are you going to tell me?" Rachel asked, sounding a little hysterical even to herself.

The girl glanced around the shop, then leaned into Rachel. "They'll find you."

It can't be true, Rachel told herself all the way home. The sky was still blue, the traffic lights turned red yellow and green. But something felt like it had been broken inside of Rachel, as if she no longer synced up to reality. The horrors – so graphically exposed – as well as the other allegations could not be true. Could they?

She shouldn't have handed over that viewer.

Rich would never believe her.

She would just have to insist they go back. She'd even forgotten the cookies.

All day she had a hard time concentrating. The images on the viewer were seared onto her brain, as awful as the film about concentration camps in the mid-20th century she'd been forced to watch in sixth grade. The faces of little children, twisted in ferocious agony or drooling under the influence of soporific drugs kept intruding onto her screens, as well as the reality of the surgeries, nauseating her.

When Rich came home from work that evening, she waited until Sam went to sleep to bring out the PVD from the clinic. As she settled into her favorite chair, she brought up something that had occurred to her earlier. "How come," she wanted to know, "you weren't enhanced?"

"Me?" Rich asked, startled. "It... it... uh, it never came up."

"Really?" she said. "Hm."

"No," he said. "And so what? Just because my dad didn't encourage me... isn't that even more reason to encourage Sam?"

Rachel looked up, met his eyes, wondered how he would react to the images on the MAYDAY viewer. "I don't know, Rich. I honestly don't know." She took a deep breath. "I went somewhere today... to check out... did you know there's a group called MayDay?"

"Those kooks…yes, we've heard of them. They're a real problem at some of the labs at work…they've been known to break in and destroy research. What about them?"

Rachel hesitated. "Do you know what MayDay stands for? At least the original spelling?"

"No," he replied impatiently. "And I don't care."

"I just can't believe it's as easy as they say it is, Rich. I can't believe there are no complications, no issues. I can't believe everything they're telling us, Rich. So I found this group… Moms and Dads against Enhancement. They have a… a video…a video that shows things that I think you ought to at least consider before we make a decision. Please, will you at least come with me tomorrow on the way to work? It's over on Morningside… not too far off your route, right?"

"Morningside? You went all the way over there? Are you crazy, Rachel? What if the car'd been stolen? What if you'd been jumped?"

"The neighborhood wasn't that bad," she answered. "Please, won't you just keep an open mind?"

The next morning, after the school bus came for Sam, Rich followed Rachel across town, all the way to Morningside. Before starting out, she double checked the coordinates in her GPS, then sent them to Rich's vehicle. When they arrived at Morningside, she double checked again. But it didn't seem to matter, because when they reached their destination, which was obviously the very same building as the day before, the café was closed.

In fact, it was more than closed. The building appeared deserted, vacant, the windows boarded up, the door that had been covered with advertisements and posters soaped over.

Rachel stood on the sidewalk, staring at the façade, speechless. Rich pulled up to the curb behind her. "Well?" he asked through the open window. "Where is it?"

"It…it was here," she replied, looking one way up the street then down the other. "I swear, this was the place… the address was in my GPS. There was a café right here…they had cookies and latte and…"

She turned around, in time to see him shake his head. "I asked you to keep an open mind," he said before he closed his window. "And all you can do is make shit up?"

Maybe she was hallucinating, Rachel thought as she turned to stare at the empty storefront. Was it possible she really wasn't as open minded as she wanted to think she was?

Until Sam's baseball game that Saturday, that Rich coached and Rachel attended more out of a sense of duty than anything else. She sat on the bleachers, knitting, feeling cut off from both husband and son.

"Is that your boy?" A woman with the sun glasses and a hat shading the rest of her face leaned over and touched Rachel's shoulder.

"Oh," Rachel said, startled out of her reverie. "No…that's Sam. He's at first base today… how about yours?"

"My boy's not here today," the woman answered.

Startled, ever more confused, Rachel took an even better look at the woman, and realized she was sitting so that the sun was behind her, and if Rachel tried to look at her, the light blinded her. "I'm sorry, Rachel began…

"No need to apologize. I came to see your boy today, Rachel. You live in the Harrison house, I think… we used to live on your street. My name was Carol Tyson. Now it's just Carol. 79-2044."

Rachel sat back, stunned. The woman beside her was dressed in drab sweats, her dirty-blonde hair pulled back under a baseball cap. She wore aviator sun glasses, and no jewelry at all. She looked like all the other women clustered around the bleachers. "I'm Rachel," she muttered, more out of habit.

"I know," the woman smiled, a quick tight fold of her lips that passed for a smile. "And I know you're thinking of having your boy enhanced, but please…" she gripped Rachel's arm so tightly Rachel nearly winced. "Don't." She paused, lowered her glasses enough that Rachel could see her washed-out blue eyes. "Don't do it. Not to your son, not to your family. It's not worth it. None of it is worth it."

"You mean things go wrong?" asked Rachel.

"I mean all of it is wrong. It's not really ball players they're after... The kids who get the enhancements, the soldiers... you know how they say all our battles are fought with drones, Rachel? Those drones... who fight the wars now... those are our kids.... That's what happens to the ones who don't play sports...the ones who ... who "don't make it." Of course everyone gets a contract. Because if they don't get turned into athletes, they get turned into drones."

"What?" Rachel pulled back, stared in disbelief into the woman's sunglasses, into the reflection of her own disbelief. "That's..." She broke off, glanced around. Most of the other women were watching the children, or chatting among themselves. A few were absorbed in their PCD's. But a few glanced in her direction. She glanced across the field, where the hot dog truck had set up and was offering burgers and dogs and coffee. "I need a cup of coffee. You?"

"I could do with something stronger, but sure. Let's go talk over there." Carol nodded toward the empty picnic tables under the trees on the other side of the truck.

As soon as they were away from the other parents, Rachel turned to Carol. "And your son? Is he okay?"

Carol shrugged. "Okay... he's okay. He's different." She stopped as the spring wind whipped her hair out of her scarf and around her cheeks. "He's not the same, and he'll never be." She nodded over her shoulder towards the field, where the other team had come to bat to a spattering of applause from the parents on the bleachers. "Those kids, those babies? They don't just take their legs, their feet. They take something else, something else I can't explain. Please, if there's any way around it, don't do it. Wait. Let your son decide, when he's older... even twelve, thirteen."

"It's not me so much," said Rachel, slowly. She bit her lip, looked around. Rich was positioned at first base, urging on the infield. His hair ruffled in the breeze, and except for the fact he was bigger, there wasn't much to distinguish him from the players. "It didn't help the café wasn't there when I tried to show my husband."

"We have to move around," replied Carol. "What we're doing... spreading the word, telling the truth...no one wants us to do that. No one involved, that is." She glanced over Rachel's shoulder, to the parking lot. Rachel followed her line of sight, and noticed a late-model minivan flashed its headlights three times quickly. "There's my ride." She reached out, gave Rachel a quick hug. "Just say no," she said softly.

Rachel walked over to the coffee truck, feeling sick. Out of force of habit, she ordered coffee. Her hands were shaking as she sank down on the picnic bench. A ball bounced near the table and the boy who came running over for it was Sam. "Mommy," he grinned.

Sun glinted on his freckled nose, turned the highlights in his hair red.

"Let's go!" cried Rich from across the field.

"Gotta go, Mom," he said, grabbed the ball and ran off.

She watched him run back across the sun-dappled field, whooping as he threw the ball to second base.

I don't want him to be different, she thought. Rich has to listen, he has to understand. There has to be a way. She spent the rest of the game thinking while the blue-green yarn with the gold-brown flecks spooled through her fingers and the clicking needles.

Later, when Sam had gone out for ice cream with the rest of the team, she joined Rich on the couch. The big game hadn't started yet, and he was clicking through channels. "Have you ever wondered," she asked, "why your father didn't have you enhanced?"

He looked at her with those beautiful blue-green eyes that made her heart ache. "You've already asked me that, Rachel, and you know it wasn't an option for me. They didn't do kids back then."

"Back then?" She smiled, just a little. "Back then is all of what... twenty years ago? At some point you got old enough...big enough... when you were seventeen, eighteen."

Rich put his PCD down and stared at her. "What are you trying to say, Rachel?"

"What I'm trying to say is that I don't think it's right for us to make decisions about parts of Sam he's not old enough to know whether he'll miss them or not. But I do think it could be right for you."

"Me?"

"Well, why not? You're not too old. The program began with adults, after all, and it says they accept people into their mid-thirties. You're not even 30 yet, Rich. You played baseball… you still play softball, it's been your life for as long as you've been Sam's age, right? So why not go for it?" Rachel gazed back at him steadily, holding his eyes with hers, those beautiful, blue-green eyes, flecked with orange.

"You're saying I should be the one to get enhanced? Not Sam?"

"That's exactly what I'm saying." She picked up his hand, brought it to her cheek. "Why not? The least you can do is apply."

Because visits with family members were part of the contract, Rachel wasn't surprised when a limousine pulled up in front of the house shortly after the school bus took Sam away one September morning. The leaves crunched under the tires as it swung into the drive. The driver who got out was wearing a suit, and carrying a white envelope that contained a PVD. He was young, very clean cut, and soft spoken, as he handed it to Rachel and politely asked her to come with him if she would agree to the conditions of the visit.

"I wasn't expecting a visit so soon," she said, scanning the screen.

"Your husband's having the bandages removed from his eyes today, ma'am. He requested that you be the first thing he sees."

Rachel smiled as she scrawled her initials across the screen. "Just a second," she said. She'd finished the sweater last night. It was going to be a Christmas present, but why not give it to him now? With his eyes open, he'd be able to see it, remind him of her when she wasn't there.

The driver was standing by the door of the back seat. He opened it as she locked the door. She slid inside, and he bent down, aimed a small device at her. A flash exploded in her eyes. Rachel slumped.

When she opened her eyes, the driver was still standing beside the open door. She peered outside. Somehow, they'd arrived at a brick building, with broad stone steps. "We're here? How...?"

"We're here." The driver beckoned. A nurse was standing at the top of the steps, holding a steaming cup.

"Mrs. Ingot," she smiled warmly. "Please... drink this tea? And come with me."

"Tea?" Rachel blinked. The liquid was pleasantly warm, faintly floral-smelling, and vaguely sweet with just a hint of spice. By the time she'd finished the last sip, she felt much more awake.

"Feel better?" smiled the nurse. She beckoned. "There's someone very impatient to see you."

"How's he doing," Rachel breathed, scampering to keep up.

The nurse's footsteps made almost no sound on the polished floors, but Rachel's clicked alarmingly.

"He's fabulous," she replied. "So far he's coming through spectacularly." At the door she paused, knocked twice. "Here we are, Rich, Dr. Jorgenson. Look who's here."

The figure on the bed turned his head in the direction of the door. Rachel bit her lip. She'd seen the videos of course, viewed all the required literature. She thought she'd been adequately prepared, but her knees still felt weak.

"Mrs. Ingot," boomed the doctor.

She ignored him, went swiftly to the bed, where Rich held out his hand – or what was left of it. At least the fingers were still his. She let him close the bandaged apparatus around her palm, curling her fingers through his.

"Gently now," the doctor said. "Those fingers are still in the healing stages...are we ready, Rich?"

"Absolutely," Rich whispered, squeezing Rachel's hand with a grip that nearly cut off her circulation.

"Ouch!" she cried.

"Sorry," he answered. "I'm still... learning."

"Of course you are," said Dr. Jorgenson. "Let's get these bandages off, shall we?" He picked up a pair of gleaming scissors from a tray beside the bed.

The nurse shoved a chair behind Rachel's knees and she sank into it gratefully, nursing her fingers. Rich turned his face to the doctor, who carefully began to snip. The nurse scurried to position a light over the doctor's shoulder. Rachel clutched the sweater, clinging to the thick cable stitches like a life raft. In the white hospital room, it was the only spot of color besides her own clothes.

"There," said the doctor. He dropped the thick wad of bandages into a waiting basin. "Now just a second. Let's get some of this goop off." He dabbed at Rich's eyes with a towel. "There we are. Now. There's still a fair amount of swelling, so let's take this slow. One at a time."

The seconds ticked by, told off in the beats of Rachel's heart. She could hear it beating, so hard she saw it moving beneath her chest.

"Perfect," breathed the doctor.

There was the sound of a soft whir, then a series of clicks as Rich turned his head. "Rachel," he whispered. "Rachel?"

With every ounce of courage she possessed, Rachel leaned forward, stroked his fingers, and gazed into the bulging, steel colored lens that covered his newly enhanced eyes. "I'm here, sweetheart," she managed against the nausea rising in her throat. "See?"

"Oh, my God," Rich answered, "Oh my God, Rachel, I can't believe how beautiful you really are."

Later, when he had fallen asleep, Rachel got up to leave. She had no idea how much time had passed, how long she'd spent sitting at his side, listening to him rhapsodize about all his new eyes could see. He loved the sweater, in fact, mostly because of all the minute variations in color he could now see.

"Your driver's here," the nurse announced. She'd been back and forth and in and out several times throughout Rachel's visit, checking this and that.

Rachel hesitated, leaned over Rich. She stroked his hair, kissed his forehead, and straightened the sweater he insisted on placing over his hospital blanket. With his eyes closed, he still looked exactly the way he always had.

"What a beautiful sweater," said the nurse.

"Thank you," answered Rachel. "It used to match his eyes."

The End

Conjuring Johnny Depp

(Celebrity Supernatural #1)

"I hope you're not planning anything too elaborate." Olivia's voice crackles and pops over the cell phone. Wherever she is, the reception is terrible.

"What did you say?" I scream back into my own. The jackhammer going off right outside my car door doesn't help either. "GianCarlo wants you to pick a date?" There's no way I'm going to let a milestone like my best friend's fiftieth birthday pass without some recognition. Olivia knows this and suspects I have something planned, which of course I do.

However, her attention these days is easily taken up by her latest conquest, an international businessman who so far has flown her off to meet him in Bali, Monaco and Marrakech. He tends to show up unexpectedly, always bearing wine and exquisite gifts, settling in for days of endless and exotic sex.

But there's something shifty about him that we all sense, something that plagues Olivia herself with a vague sense of unease, which is partly why I decided on this particular present. There are lots of reasons, of course, but GianCarlo is definitely one of them.

"You know perfectly well he hasn't asked me to pick a date. I said, I don't want you doing anything EE-LAB-BOR--" The rest dissolves into static fuzz. I smile and gently press END.

If she's in traffic, she might babble on for minutes before she even realizes we're not connected any more. It isn't nice of me, I know, but there's too much to do before the coven meeting to waste a minute of it lying to the guest of honor. Besides, I know once Olivia realizes the birthday surprise I'm planning, she'll be too speechless to object.

I murmur the traffic spell I only use when I need life to flow especially smoothly and find myself running through my list of chores with the efficiency of someone whose elementals have achieved harmonic congruence. At least those are the words Olivia uses to describe the world when things are going particularly well for her. As they appear to be now.

But as we all know, appearances can be deceiving.

I turn the corner into the parking lot of the Weirdly Ways and Curious Goods shop that Olivia's ex--our small town's most small-minded minister--condemned regularly from his pulpit. Olivia's become the woman I want to be: strong-minded and independent and passionate about everything. She went through hell before, during and after her divorce due to her vindictive ex and his similarly closed-minded congregation. Sometimes, I still wonder why Olivia didn't just move. But she has a life here, Olivia always answers, whenever she's asked why she stays, and she loves our small town tucked midway between Boston and New York. So she hasn't left... at least, not yet.

On the one hand, GianCarlo seems perfect--the absolute opposite of her close-minded ex.

But on the other...he's just too… smooth.

It's not for me to make the decision, of course. I just think I've hit upon a way to help her--not to mention a mind-blowing birthday present.

I enter the shop with my list in hand. Dark red candles, of course, like Olivia's Scottish heroine hair, and purple, her favorite color. And black for protection and pink to help manifest a miracle in service of the highest good.

Which is what we're going to need, I think, if this is going to work. I buy new smudge sticks of white sage and sweet-grass, incense in jasmine and patchouli, and essential oils in every type of rose I can find. And honeysuckle, to bind the spell. I tuck all my purchases in the dainty willow basket and take them to the register.

"Hey there, girlfriend," says Clarice behind the counter. Her blue eyes are huge and fringed with long dark lashes. "I thought this was a half-century celebration. This stuff looks more like a love spell. What are we doing, conjuring up some sex god to give Olivia a birthday thrill?"

"Something like that." I smile. I don't want to give too much away, for there's power in secrets. If there's power in the words that get spoken, there's even more in the ones that don't. The fact that it's a paradox tells you that it's the truth.

At least that's what Olivia says. She's the one who introduced me to the coven. I'd been a stumbling solitary, reading every Cunningham and Conway I could get my hands on, when I happened to meet Olivia at a psychic fair. She saw me for the poor lost lamb that I was, and taking me under her wing, taught me more about the true meaning of Divine Power than all the nuns at Mount St. Joseph Academy combined.

And tonight--tonight, I'm determined to show her exactly how much I've learned, and how much our friendship means to me.

———

I say goodbye to Clarice and head toward the town cemetery with a renewed sense of purpose. The story in the newspaper last week made me think that such a thing as I was planning might be possible. An ancient Englishman had shown up at the Town Hall, claiming that a woman whom everyone had known locally as Letty Kosloski was really his sister, one Lady Elizabeth Batstow.

Apparently a long time resident of our small town - Aaron Kosloski -had spent some time as a gamekeeper on one of those Downton Abbey estates in pre-World War II Britain. He fell for Elizabeth in a bad way, and when he'd been banished back to the U.S., along with whatever else they did to gamekeepers back then who weren't in D.H. Lawrence novels, he somehow managed bring her to America.

In England, it was said that she'd vanished into thin air.

The youngest brother had never forgotten the mystery of what happened to his oldest sister, and he'd traced her at last to our quiet corner of Connecticut. The fact that she was dead didn't deter him; he'd come armed with an order for disinterment. The whole town was abuzz with the story, for Letty Kosloski appeared as ordinary as an old shoe. But Aaron Kosloski was Native American on his mother's side, and both Olivia and I knew him to be a shamanic practitioner, secretive as they come.

I'm here to take some dirt from Letty's grave. Just yesterday the press announced the results of the DNA testing. Letty Kosloski, whose weather-beaten face and accent-less American offered no suggestion of a lineage any more storied than Olivia's rescued mutt, was beyond all shadow of a doubt an English lady to the manor born.

I trudge up the path that winds between the graves, and it's easy to see Letty's. The opened grave is a dark gash against the green, and beside it, a muddy mound sags sadly into the long grass.

I peer into the empty hole. Rainwater's pooled in the bottom, and I feel the soft edge give way beneath my shoe. I stumble back and nearly trip over Aaron's headstone. Reading between the lines, I'm sure I discern some accusation of foul play involving the "black" arts. Their children staunchly maintain that their mother never mentioned a life in England, and in fact, never even claimed to be English.

But no one really knew the Kosloskis, and there always was all that talk about Aaron and his ways. It was Aaron who first taught Olivia. She credits him for saving her soul, and if that's true, then he just as surely has had a hand in saving mine. So he's my spiritual grandfather, in a sense.

I pluck a bright yellow sunflower from the bunch and place it gently in front of Aaron's stone. "Grandfather," I whisper. I ask for his assistance, and assure any spirits that might be listening that I intend nothing but the highest good for all concerned. I feel a little swell rise up from the ground beneath my feet and the air surrounding me thickens almost imperceptibly. I feel a gentle stroke like a feather down the back of my neck, and the softest kiss of a breeze on my cheek. "Thank you," I say.

I whisper a similar little prayer over the hole where Letty's body rested. Enough of her essence has gone into the earth, after twenty years, I think, to be effective. She'd been buried in a plain pine box that had almost splintered apart when it was raised.

I gently place a trowel-full in a zip-lock freezer bag. I throw the flowers into the grave, and they land at the bottom with a splash, and float for a few moments before they disappear. It pleases me to think my offering's been accepted and as I turn to leave, I think I smell the scent of burning sweet-grass on the wet wind.

———

"And I told you not to do anything elaborate," says Olivia the minute she walks into the house and smells the fifty roses in all shades from vermilion to coral to cream that are artfully arranged in the living room amidst the fifty white candles. "You're a dear, you know that?" She grabs me in a fierce hug, and for a single moment I wonder if there's *any* possibility she might be less than happy about what I have planned, and then I dismiss the thought.

The doorbell rings. I hurry to answer it. The rest of the coven is right on time. They know tonight is a special night because of the birthday, and since most of them have found an excuse to either phone or stop by Clarice's shop, all of them have heard about my purchases.

Even Leslie, a lawyer who gave up her career as a prosecutor to represent abused children, arrives on time, tearing off her threadbare power suit as she heads into the bathroom to change into her preferred after-work attire. She's the only one who always wears comfy sweats. The rest of us tend to dress according to whatever mood and weather seem to dictate, and tonight, all of us are in black, with touches of scarlet and gold, fuschia and orange, as if by prearrangement.

Marnie and her sister Karen come together; Jasmina, our wise-woman herbalist who teaches belly-dancing at the JCC, and Clarice nearly trip over each other when the porch light inexplicably bursts over Karen's head just as she crosses the threshold. "The energy's jumping right out the door," says Jasmina. "What exactly do you have planned?"

"Just a little birthday present," I say, as I retrieve a new bulb. I swirl it in salt and rub a little honeysuckle oil on it, whispering my intention that only beings of love and light should pass beneath its gleam. A sudden gust of wind sets russet leaves swirling at my ankles and the candles in the jack-o-lantern flare and spit. Jasmina's right, I think. The energy is jumping.

Leslie comes back from the bathroom in black sweats and pale pink socks. "Are we doing gifts before or after?"

"After, right?" says Marnie. "With the cake." I used to think that Marnie was a hopeless control freak, and then I realized that structure gives her security and she just feels better when she knows what's coming next.

"Well," I hesitate. I know I have to tell them sooner or later and it seems better to explain things before we begin, rather than during. Incredulity can stop a ritual cold. "I think we better do gifts first."

"Then I'll be right back," says Leslie. She dashes off into the night in her stocking feet and I know she's probably forgotten shoes and can't stand the thought of shoving her swollen feet into her work pumps. I remember there're sneakers in the closet she can wear home, but Marnie is demanding to know why custom should be breached, and Olivia is looking at me even more closely than before.

"Come on in, everyone." I lead the way into the living room, where I've arranged lavender and pale pink satin and velvet pillows inside a carefully chalked pentacle. Between the candles and the flowers and the fire in the fireplace, the whole scene elicits oohs and aahs. "I'd just prefer to do gifts first, if you don't mind. The ceremony itself--that's my gift. I wrote it just for you, Olivia. So if you don't mind, I'd like to finish with it."

"Why, sure," says Karen, always the mediator between Marnie's moods and the rest of us. She smiles deliberately at her sister and Marnie subsides. The front door slams and Leslie comes in, looking cold.

"The wind's really picking up out there," she says. "Feels like something big's brewing. Kelly, how likely it is one of those trees is going to come down on a car?"

A sudden gust roars down the fireplace and the flames leap up. "Feels like something big's brewing right here, Kelly," says Olivia. "Come on, what gives?"

"Okay," I say. "You're right. I do have something special planned." I hesitate and take a deep breath. This is beyond anything we've ever attempted as a coven.

Jasmina, on my left, gives my forearm a gentle nudge. "What're you up to, Kelly?" Her soft Jamaican lilt intensifies. "You look like the goose that wants to lay the golden egg. So do it, before you burst, woman."

I look around the circle, at each woman in turn. When I get to Olivia I smile. "We're going to conjure Johnny Depp."

There is a split second of shocked silence, and then they all start talking at once.

"What do you mean, conjure him? Bring him here?"

"Are you kidding?"

"Are you crazy?"

"Yum, yum, yum. Johnny Depp." That's from Leslie.

But it's Olivia's reaction that stings. "Kelly, honey, you really are crazy, aren't you?"

"I'm absolutely dead serious, Olivia. And I'm surprised you, of all people, would think that such a thing's impossible." To her credit, she looks taken aback. "You're an amazing woman, Olivia. You've come out of one of the toughest things I've seen anyone go through, and you're not only not defeated, you're positively radiant." I feel the tears spring to my eyes, and my throat starts to swell. "I wanted to give you something really, truly special for your birthday--an experience you'll never forget--"

She'll never forget being charged with kidnapping if we *are* successful," says Leslie. "Or have you forgotten that part?"

"I don't intend to kidnap him," I reply. "We're not going to hold him here against his will."

"I know Johnny Depp has a reputation for being quirky," puts in Jasmina. "But I don't think even the quirkiest person would appreciate being poofed out of his own life and plunked into ours without some kind of warning or consent. Do you?" She pins me with a penetrating look.

"What even makes you can work such a thing?" asks Marnie.

"Theoretically, it's possible," says Clarice, before I can answer. I bless her for all the hours she spends reading the books she sells. Most of it sticks and for a writer like me, she is an invaluable resource, sort of a cross between Google and an encyclopedia. "There are native traditions that say it's possible to walk between the worlds, and even lead others through. But only a powerful shaman can do it."

"Or one who's already been lead through," I finish. Our eyes lock and I know a moment of true *deja vu*. We'd had this conversation when the first articles appeared.

"No wonder you've been asking so many questions about Letty and Aaron," says Olivia.

"You didn't disagree with my theory, though, did you?" I look at Clarice. I'm not backing down. I know, somehow, that this is the right thing to do, crazy as it may seem. Maybe I am crazy. Crazy people do crazy things, but that doesn't necessarily mean they're not the right things to do. "Let's give it a try, okay? I've put an awful lot of thought and energy into this. And maybe it won't work anyway." The candlelight is kind to our aging faces, the shadows gently gray in the peachy glow.

I see a subtle longing flicker across every face, a wish, a hope, a dream as fleeting as the sudden gust that roars down the chimney, as real as

Don Juan de Marco and his world of ideas. They exchange glances, shrug, nod and smile.

Olivia looks at me and in her eyes, I see what might be a smidgeon of hope. "We have to be prepared for it not to work."

"But then again," says Clarice softly, as the rest settle back. "Maybe it will."

————

Afterwards I'm sure it's the doubt that defeats us. Olivia lingers after the others leave, Leslie still wearing my sneakers. "You know," she says, leaning into the glow of the new porch light, "maybe it's just as well. What was I supposed to do with him, anyway?"

I smile. "An' it harm none, do as ye will. What kind of a witch are you?"

"Not a very good one, obviously," she replies. We look at each other and I start to cry. "Oh, don't cry, honey, this is probably the cutest thing anyone's ever tried to do for me."

"Really?" I squeak against her damp silk shoulder.

"Really." She pats my back and sets me upright. "That whole Don Juan de Marco idea--with the real Johnny Depp? Who wouldn't want that for a birthday present? You should get some sleep. You were glowing like a blowtorch for quite a while in there."

"Yeah?" Olivia sees auras. She says anyone can see them, but I don't. "What color was mine?"

"White and gold, mostly. Pink, in the center." She kisses my cheek and in the shadowed depths of her huge purse, her cell phone begins to blink red. That's new, I think. She never used to carry it with her. She turns to leave, fluttering a farewell over her shoulder. "GianCarlo? Ciao, bello! Where are you? Home? My home? You're here?" Her feet crunch through ankle deep leaves as she disappears, giggling like a schoolgirl into the darkness.

"Good night, Olivia," I whisper. "Happy birthday." Watching her sashay down the path, pink pashmina swaying, I know no one would ever believe that a little over three years ago, her husband of twenty-seven years had been accused of molesting a series of little girls in the church where he'd been a minister.

Buddy Love's wet nose brings me back to reality. "Okay, boys," I say. "Let's go out."

The magic words take them to the kitchen, but something makes Duffy's ears prick up and he growls the moment he enters the room.

"What's wrong, boy?" I ask. Just don't let it be another mouse, I think, as I switch on the lights. Duffy chased the last mouse right up Marnie's leg. I'd have to die if that happened to me. I switch the light on, but there's nothing running in any direction and Duffy's gaze is fixed directly on the back door.

I grab the cordless phone when Duffy's chest goes down, his tail goes low and he growls again. The growl alerts Buddy Love. The kitchen door is locked. I tiptoe to the window and peek over the tops of the unbleached muslin curtains.

The night is still now; whatever storm blew through before the ritual is over. Beside me, Buddy Love whines and Duffy growls. "What is it, boy?" I ask. My heart pounds in my chest. There is something out there--something alien and strange--but Buddy Love is whining and scratching at the door.

I check to make sure 911 is punched into the phone, and with my finger on the CALL button, I open the kitchen door. The dogs immediately begin to howl, and I realize that if I hadn't been so cautious, I might've tripped over the naked man lying just outside the door.

I hush the dogs and tiptoe forward. He's asleep, as soundly asleep as I would imagine it's possible for a human to be, and naked as the day he was born. A shock of honey blond hair falls over his face and I push it back gently with a shaking hand, revealing dark brown roots.

He rolls over on his side, and as I stare down the entire length of his body, alabaster as marble in the yellowish light, I know that the sleeping naked man on my back porch is undeniably, indisputably, Johnny Depp.

———

It takes me the better part of an hour to drag him into the middle of my kitchen. At first I hesitate to touch him too firmly. The last thing I want to do is wake him. Everyone will be more rational in the morning, I think, because Leslie's warnings about kidnapping suddenly have a whole new meaning. It would probably be good to talk to Leslie before he even wakes up, and I wonder how early might be too early.

But the dead weight of a grown man is a lot for me to handle on my own and finally I have to grab him by the ankles and pull him flat on his back over the bump in the kitchen door. Sweat's running down my sides by the time I get him as far as half way across the floor.

I catch a glimpse of myself in the stainless steel surface of the fridge. I look like a goddess of war, with my hair sticking up in all directions and my black sweater drenched and sticking to my back. I want to strip down to my bra, at least, but don't dare, for fear he might charge me with attempted rape as well as kidnapping if he comes to and sees himself naked and me all sweaty in my underwear.

And who would ever believe my side of it? He is quite delicious. The boys retreat to their hideout under the kitchen table and at last I have him positioned as comfortably as I dare.

I grab a quilt intended for my guest room, gently tuck it over him, and put a throw pillow from my couch under his head. "Come on, boys." I breathe a little prayer that this all be some weird hallucination brought about the combination of the candles and the incense and the phases of the moon and follow the boys up to bed.

———

In the night I convince myself that Johnny, like the ghost of Jacob Marley, is most likely the result of too much poorly digested cheese. It's not until I find him curled up under my quilt sleeping soundly as a newborn, the dogs joyfully licking his face, that I remember that Scrooge was wrong about the connection between the ghost and the cheese.

As the dogs finish their business in the poop patch, I hear the front doorbell ring, and they bound barking into the house, even as I tiptoe past Johnny's prone body.

To my amazement, it's Leslie, sleeves already rolled up. She's got a brown paper bag in her hand. "Here you go," she says, and turns to leave. "I'd stay but I'm due at a depo--"

"No, Leslie." I grab at her hand. "Wait--there's something... something wrong--"

"Wrong shoes?" she asks, instant concern creased across her forehead.

"D-do you have just a couple minutes?" I sag weakly against the doorframe. Something about seeing her in the cold daylight, in her dusty black suit and carefully applied makeup, makes me feel rather the way I imagine the witch from the Wizard of Oz felt when she looked up and saw the house falling on her.

"What's wrong, honey?" She looks at me more closely. "Are you okay?"

"J-just come in a minute," I say. The draft claws at my ankles and I can only imagine how cold the hard kitchen floor is.

Leslie watches me warily as I lead the way to the kitchen. "Kelly, can you please give me some idea--" She stops short as I stand aside to let her see Johnny's sleeping body. The boys are sitting beside him, tongues hanging out, tails softly brushing across the floor. Since he's clearly no immediate threat, they've decided to give him a chance.

"Leave him alone," I hiss, as Buddy Love bends down and sniffs experimentally at Johnny's neck. Johnny sighs and shifts, but doesn't wake.

Leslie grips my biceps with an iron clasp and says, "Please tell me that's not who I think that person looks like."

There's not much I can do but shrug helplessly.

"Sonuvabitch," she swears under her breath. "Kelly, life's not a movie. What do you think he's going to do when he wakes up?" Again, I can only shrug, though I can feel the tears starting to well up behind my eyes. "You think he's going to be *happy* about this? You think he's going to fall in love with one of us? He's not a character in a movie--he's a *person* with a life. You can't just--hijack--people... even if you did use..."

She breaks off and shakes her head. "You know, I went along with it last night because--well, because I never in a million years believed you'd actually be able to physically manifest his body." She pauses. "How can someone who would even dream of doing anything like this call herself an ethical witch?" She snaps out a cell phone, punches a single number, then stalks back down the hall, the echo of her heels hollow as death knells.

Do not ask for whom the bell tolls. My mother's voice rises ominously out of my memory. *It tolls for thee.*

Shut up, mother, I think, as I overhear Leslie say into the cell phone, "Amanda? Yeah, it's me. Look, you're going to have tell Rahim he's got to cover the Henderson deposition this morning. Something's come up. Something big. Yeah, I'm involved. Yeah, it could be bad. Yeah, I will. Thanks, you're a peach." She flips the phone closed. "You know, it would be bad enough if he was just some--some nobody off the streets of some podunk town east of Bumblefuck. But, oh, no, you had to go and conjure up someone who's only known to millions of people. What do you think's going to happen when he wakes up? You don't think he'll be *amused*, do you?" She passes me shaking her head. "We have to call Clarice. She helped you with this, didn't she?"

"Not specifically. She just gave me some ideas. Pointed me in the right direction, so to speak."

Leslie is standing at Johnny's feet. He's flat on his back now, a slight smile on his face. There's the merest haze of a beard on his chin in the white wash of light, and he clutches a corner of the quilt with one hand. "How much for this quilt?" she whispers.

"What?" I don't think I've heard her correctly.

"How much… for the quilt. The quilt he's under. I want it."

"Just help me get out of this and it's yours." Our eyes lock and the bargain's made.

She shifts a bit on her feet and when she talks, her tone is different, crisp, and lawyerly. "How long's he been asleep?"

"Since I found him last night on the porch."

"He was on the porch?"

"Literally on the doorstep. I had to drag him in here."

"And he didn't wake up?"

I shake my head.

"Hm. That's odd. Is he naked under there?"

I nod. "As a jaybird."

"No, seriously?" She doesn't sound quite so lawyerly.

"Oh, yeah. He's naked. Look--he's having a real nice dream." I point to where a little pup tent is rising at the level of his groin.

Leslie covers her mouth with a little gasp. "Kelly Sabatelli, I just can't believe you'd actually do something like this."

"You know, I've been thinking," I say defensively. "All your talk of hi-jacking and kidnapping--what makes you think he didn't want to come--he didn't agree?"

For a moment Leslie is silent. Then she motions me out of the kitchen. The dogs continue their vigil. She puts an arm around my shoulders, and speaks to me in the same tone of voice used to calm frightened children and raving lunatics. "You know, Kelly, he's not his characters."

In the hallway, I pause and look at her, and I think how beautiful the colors are swirling in the depths of her eyes and I wonder when the last time was that anyone told her so. Don Juan de Marco was right about that, too. Every woman should be told that the colors in her eyes are beautiful. Every day. But all I say is, "Oh, no, Leslie. See, that's where I think you're wrong. I think on some level, he is his characters--every one of them. He has to be, in the same way I'm all mine."

I think, for a split second that Leslie gets it, she really gets it, but then she shakes her head and the spell is broken. She gives me a little push. "Go call Clarice, and tell her to get her butt over here ASAP."

"Where're you going?" I ask.

"I'll just keep an eye on Mr. Depp while he sleeps."

"While he dreams," I say with a smirk and she only answers me with a look that would freeze rain and a blush that would stop traffic.

———

Once word gets around that Weirdly Ways is closed due to an emergency, it doesn't take long for the coven to gather, except for Olivia, whom I have to assume is tied up, maybe literally, with GianCarlo, and possibly for days.

By two o'clock we're sitting around Johnny, three on each side. The strong afternoon light is not at all as kind as the candlelight last night, and we look like some Stepfordized version of Macbeth's Three Weird Sisters and their understudies. He's still sound asleep. He snores every so often, shifts position, and even drools a couple times. The sleep is deeply unnatural, but he seems normal enough.

"He is so beautiful," Marnie coos. Her hands flutter in her lap and I know she wants to peek under the blanket. I told her to go ahead and look, but Karen's shock has so far kept her under control. I'm not sure she will be able to resist, however, if he starts dreaming again. "You mean you found him on your back porch and moved him in here and the boys have been noisy all day, and he hasn't so much as stirred?"

"He's stirred, all right," says Leslie.

"But he doesn't wake up," I finish immediately, lest she whet their appetites unwittingly.

"That's pretty strange, don't you think?" says Marnie.

"Well, it's obvious this isn't a natural sleep," says Jasmina.

"It's an enchanted sleep," says Marnie.

Karen comes in from the living room, where my tiny TV is tuned to CNN. "Um--there was just a segment on that Johnny Depp's been reported missing on the set of his latest film. Seems he just vanished. Into thin air." Her mouth is a thin, tense line.

"Well. I guess that answers that." Leslie looks like she's bitten a lemon.

"We have to get Olivia here," says Clarice pointedly at me.

"But GianCarlo showed up last night. What if he's taken her off to Fuji or Kilimanjaro or--"

Jasmina puts her arm around me. "We have to find her."

"She's the one you conjured him for," Leslie says.

"She's the focus of the spell," says Clarice. "I really don't think it can be broken without her."

"What if he wakes up before we can find her?" asks Karen.

"I think we have a bigger problem if he doesn't," says Jasmina. She folds her arms across her chest, and looks at each of us in turn. "If he doesn't wake up, he won't eat. If he doesn't eat, he'll starve. If he continues to sleep much longer, we're going to have to get him hooked up to some sort of IV, just to make sure he stays hydrated."

A low muffled sound comes from underneath the quilt, and a moment later, Marnie sniffs. "Oh my God, I think he farted."

The whole ridiculous absurdity of the entire situation collapses on top of me like a house of cards and I start to giggle softly, crumpling against Jasmina. "I feel like I'm living out that old joke about the priest who skips Mass and goes to play golf on Sunday morning, and God lets him hit eighteen holes-in-one... because who is the priest ever going to be able to tell about it?" I giggle until the tears spill down my cheeks.

"We could take pictures," begins Marnie.

"No!" Leslie says in a whisper that's as close to a bellow as it's possible for a whisper to be. "No pictures." She looks at Clarice. "So you agree with me, we need Olivia here?"

Clarice exchanges a glance with me. "She was the focus, right?"

And miserably, I can only nod.

During the ride over to Olivia's house, since calling her is pointless, Jasmina asks me gently, "And just exactly why was it you thought conjuring Johnny Depp would be a good idea?"

"It was to help her make her up her mind about GianCarlo," I say. The sheer awful stupidity of what I've done is crashing on me like a jetty's worth of boulders and I can hardly lift my head out of the pit between my shoulderblades. The situation can only get worse from this point, I've decided. "Or about anyone, for that matter." At that they all turn and look at me, even Karen, who's driving. "It was that scene in Don Juan de Marco that gave me the idea--well, it was the whole movie, really. Olivia's been so tied up into knots over this GianCarlo thing from the beginning--"

"You thought an experience with Johnny Depp would help her make her up mind?" Marnie, whose vivid fits of imagination frequently exceed even mine, sounds puzzled.

"Well--" I shrug. "Isn't that what the movie was about? Don Juan de Marco? That we can imagine our lives? Our loves? And that's how we create the lives we want, by first imagining them?"

They're looking at me dubiously and I know they don't understand. Even I don't understand any more. Because what I keep struggling with, even though I know I've done a terrible thing, is the feeling that it's all going to turn out okay.

———

Olivia comes to the door looking flushed, hair wet. She's just gotten out of the shower, and GianCarlo has just fallen asleep. From the rings under her dark eyes, I can tell it's been a busy nearly twenty-four hours. To her credit, she takes one look at all of us, grabs her purse and heads for the door. "The man doesn't stop," she says, as we bundle her into the car. "He's come around twelve times in the last sixteen hours. I don't know where he gets the stamina."

"How much Viagra does that take?" asks Karen.

"He doesn't need Viagra," says Olivia. "He's amazing."

"Aren't you sore?" asks Jasmina.

Olivia blushes. "A bit. He's not at all rough, though. Just--"

"Persistent?" finishes Marnie.

Persistent, I think. I wonder if Johnny's still asleep.

"Are you going to tell me what all this is about," she asks abruptly.

"Remember last night?" says Leslie.

Olivia glances at me and I smile back weakly. "What about last night?"

We turn into my driveway and Karen parks the car.

"Come on in, Olivia," I say, as I struggle out of the car. "I have a big surprise."

———

Clarice, bless her heart, has the presence of mind to find a camera--despite Leslie's injunction--and so we have a wonderful shot of Olivia's face frozen in the moment when she looks down at my kitchen floor and sees Buddy Love and Duffy guarding Johnny Depp. Leslie's behind her, arms crossed like a storm trooper, Marnie's grinning like a demented elf, and I'm clearly cringing behind Jasmina.

The sex and the lack of sleep and the sight is all too much for her, and Olivia's knees buckle. We decamp to my living room, where Clarice has tea waiting. As the early evening sun begins to slant over the couches, it's soon apparent we've no idea what to do next.

"I think we have to try to wake him," says Jasmina. "If he continues to sleep, he'll dehydrate. We don't want to be accused of murder on top of kidnapping, after all."

"And if he wakes up," says Leslie. "We have a chance of explaining Kelly's idea to him. And maybe he is quirky enough to be reasonable about this. Though what there is to be reasonable about... I guess that's another topic for discussion."

Olivia hasn't said much, and now she leans forward. "Kelly?"

"I'm sorry," I say, the tears starting to drip down my face. "I guess it really was an awful idea--I didn't think it through. It was just--I thought if you knew for sure that GianCarlo makes you feel the way Johnny Depp makes you feel--then you'd know. You'd be able to see past all the trips and the jewelry and the stuff--and know if he was the right one for you. You've been through so much--I don't want you to waste your time or your energy on someone who isn't going to give you everything you deserve."

"Oh, honey," she says. We're all crying now, even Leslie, and Karen starts passing around the tissues.

"Hey," Marnie says, as she blows her nose. "I have an idea. His sleeping--we all agree it's not normal sleep, right?" As we all nod, she continues, "He's under an enchantment--like Sleeping Beauty. That's why he's asleep. And in the fairy tales, when you want someone to wake up, you kiss them, right?"

"You also kiss the toad to turn him into a prince," says Karen.

"I think Johnny's already a prince," says Jasmina. "What if kissing him turns him into a toad?"

"Maybe we shouldn't do anything that might turn him into a toad," says Leslie. "I don't even want to think of the legal ramifications of turning a film star worth millions and millions, with obligations worth millions and millions, into a reptile."

"An amphibian," says Clarice. "Toads are amphibians."

For a long strange moment, a twisted ribbon of a story unfurls in my head - Johnny Depp turns into a toad, his fans scream for my blood. Olivia herself lights the logs at the foot of my stake. I shake my head, take a deep breath and tell myself to stop being silly.

"It's worth a shot, though," says Marnie. "Isn't it?"

"Can't you just figure out a way to reverse the spell, Kelly?" asks Karen.

"That's going to take some time." I shred a rose petal between my fingers. It's deep dark red, the same color as fresh blood.

"Go kiss him," says Leslie. "It's worth a shot."

"Maybe we shouldn't," says Karen. "Isn't that kind of a violation?"

"I don't think it's really any more of a violation than bringing him here in the first place," replies Leslie.

"Naked, even," adds Jasmina.

"So who gets to kiss him?" Marnie looks as if she'd be glad to volunteer.

"I think it has to be Olivia," I say. "After all, I brought him here for her."

———

The light has long since faded and the kitchen is bathed in grayish gloom. The boys wag their tails listlessly when we enter. Since he's clearly not a toy, they've decided he's some sort of couch, and have snuggled up around him.

I shoo them away and we kneel in a circle, Olivia on one side of his head, and me on the other. She leans way over and gives him a chaste peck on the forehead. Nothing happens. She tries his cheek. Again, nothing.

Leslie takes a deep breath and Marnie, next to Olivia, gives her a nudge. "Oh, just go for it. Put a big wet one on that beautiful sensitive mouth."

She looks at me. "It's worth a try," I say.

But she hesitates. She smoothes his hair back from his face, caresses his cheek with the back of her hand. "I can't believe you really did this," she says. "All for me. Thank you."

Suddenly my throat is too thick to whisper anything but, "Happy birthday."

She smiles at me then, and I believe she understands. She leans over and gently touches his mouth with hers, and then, imperceptibly, presses harder, until at last, it's a kiss, a real kiss, and there on my kitchen floor, my fifty-year-old friend Olivia is actually kissing Johnny Depp, and as she pulls away and begins to open her eyes, he opens his.

And vanishes.

———

We order out for pizza because we can't imagine talking about what's happened in public. The delivery man looks bewildered when Marnie grabs him in a bear hug as the announcement that Johnny Depp's alive and well comes on the television just as the poor guy's giving her change, and he becomes ositively worried when we all cheer.

Again, Olivia lingers after all the others have gone home. "All's well that ends well," I say as I hand her the pink pashmina. "Johnny's back on his set--our lives are back to normal--you're going back to GianCarlo."

But she's silent until she's at the door.

"Aren't you?" I ask. She's been very quiet all night, I realize. And there've been no calls from GianCarlo.

"I'm going back to kiss GianCarlo," she says. Johnny's pillow is clutched to her chest, carefully wrapped. "To see if he makes me feel the way Johnny did. When I kissed him in the middle of your kitchen floor."

The End

FINDING SOUTHSIDE JOHNNY
(WITH DON GOODMAN)

———

CELEBRITY SUPERNATURAL #2

I **find the photograph** in the last file I remove from the bottom drawer of my desk. The file is labeled "music." It contains the picture and a manila envelope the years have sealed shut. Both are from a time in my life I don't think about.

I pause in my packing under the baleful stare of Margie, the Under-Grumpen-Uber-Fuhrer, as I like to call her. Everyone else calls her Preston the office manager's executive secretary, emphasis on the word "executive."

From her post at the doorway, Margie coughs discreetly, but I ignore her. Let the bitch wait a minute or two longer for her cigarette break. In the time I've been one of the firm's top-producing financial advisors, she's done nothing but make my work life a living hell, ever since I rejected her at my first office Christmas party. Despite the fact she dresses like a Sunday school teacher and acts prissier than a nun, the cigarette odor wafting off her flowery dress is worse than the inside of a chimney.

I take a good look at the picture. It's a black and white glossy eight by ten. A much younger version of myself looks back. I am holding a guitar and staring into space at some point beyond the photographer's shoulder. Beside me is Southside Johnny, of Southside Johnny and the Asbury Jukes. He's holding a microphone in one hand and a beer bottle in the other.

The smell of Margie's cigarettes reminds me of the musty studio's stale air. I know that in the photograph, I'm looking at the drummer, waiting for my cue. He's waiting for Johnny to finish his beer. I can feel the pressure of the guitar strings and the poise of the plastic pick between my calloused fingers, and the tension between my shoulder blades that I don't mess up this audition.

Margie coughs again, this time not so discreetly, and taps her wrist watch pointedly. "Hurry it up, Dan," she mouths.

Fuck you, I want to say. But I don't. I put the photograph back in the file, and the file on top of the last carton I carry to my car.

Preston walks me out into the humid July air. He stays fresh as a Ken doll as he assures me HR will be in touch with all the proper forms.

I want to say "Fuck you" to Preston, too, but I don't. There's a bitter taste in my mouth that seems to have sealed my tongue to the roof of my mouth, my lips to each other.

At least he doesn't offer to shake my hand. He walks back to the building, his polished loafers clicking across the steaming asphalt. He leaves me standing beside my car, feeling almost as stunned as the day just a couple weeks ago, when, after nearly thirty years of running portfolios with prudence and proper care, I made a bad call.

A spectacularly bad call as it turned out. A stock I thought just couldn't fail turned out to be riddled with fraud. I heard the news too late to stop the death spiral, and watched helplessly as balances evaporated in account after account, including, unfortunately, my own.

I shouldn't have been surprised when Preston and Margie showed up at my door with cardboard boxes in their hands. It's only surprising it took the Powers-That-Be who run the firm so long to decide my fate.

I put the carton on the front seat and get behind the wheel. I had started to believe that the Powers-That-Be were in a mood to overlook my error and give me another chance.

Stupid me.

I rip off my tie and toss it into the back seat.

Before I buckle on the seat belt, I open up the music file. This time, I carefully peel apart the edges of the manila envelope. Inside I find five or six ivory-colored guitar picks, each with a tiny version of my senior yearbook photo on one side. They were a graduation gift from my first guitar teacher, the last from a pack of a hundred or so. I'd thought them all long gone.

The envelope also contains a dozen or so thin sheets of yellowed onion skin, lined with stanzas and my crude attempts at musical notations. My songs.

A road not taken if ever there were one, I think. I press the edges of the envelope back together. I have no wish to revisit those memories, especially not now I've spattered myself like a cartoon character onto a brick wall. I happen to glance at the photograph again, and I remember it was Sam who took the picture.

Sam. Shit, I think. Sam's my oldest friend. We don't see each other much – it's been at least five years since we met in Manhattan for lunch - but we talk on the phone from time to time. The last time was when I was flush with my great idea to buy as much ADKG – the wonder stock - as possible.

I should reach out to Sam, I think. I've been too busy – all right, too scared. I'll call, I tell myself. As soon as I get home. As soon as I gather my courage. It's not yet 9:30 in the morning, but I head straight for what is about to become the best investment I ever made.

A little over a year ago, June, the bartender/hostess at my favorite watering hole, approached me for the last ten grand she needed to buy the bar. She's been paying me back at the rate of five hundred a month and since my stock debacle, especially, I've come to think of the place as my home-away-from-home. I go through the back door and find June in the office, doing her books. "Junie-tunes," I say. "Help."

She looks up in mid key-stroke, peering at me over her reading glasses like an owl. "Jesus," she says, "let me get you a drink."

I follow her into the bar and drink as much vodka as she is willing to feed me. At some point I show her the photograph. At some point I tell her the story of how I'd come to meet Southside, how it had happened that a preppy kid from the Philadelphia Main Line had run into a Jersey bar band like the Jukes. At some point I tell the story over and over again, to whoever is willing to listen and look at my picture. I never open my envelope of songs.

I drink all the vodka I can, until I finally go home to an empty house and a sheriff's sale notice tacked on the door.

More stuff happened in between, of course.

I just don't remember it very clearly. By the time I emerge from my vodka-induced fog, a couple months have passed. I'm down to my last thousand dollars. The banks take most of what we had and Karen, my soon-to-be-ex-wife, takes the rest. My son goes back to college not speaking to me, even though his college funds remain intact. I have a guitar, my books, my clothes and a car.

I start listening to Southside Johnny with a renewed appreciation for the desperation in his songs.

"So what are you going to do?" June asks me, late one night in September. The day started off warm, but the night air has a nip. I have no desire to go back to the big chilly box I'm moving out of tomorrow.

"I've been thinking about Sam," I say. I know Sam acted on my advice...I'd said I was a hundred percent sure the stock was a great investment. I sometimes still can't believe how wrong I turned out to be.

"What about Sam?" June is tidying up. It's long past closing time but she's stopped expecting me to leave. Some nights I just sleep on the back bench with the thick cushion behind the pool table. It's convenient when I wake up and want another drink.

"I think I have to go say I'm sorry in person. I can't bring myself to call. I can't write a letter, or send an email...that's too cold. I look at what I did to my life... I can't imagine what I've done to Sam's. Sam's the reason I met Southside Johnny in the first place, how I even had a shot of an audition...Sam's friendship has meant ...everything ...to me." That this is true surprises me.

June pauses in the middle of polishing a glass. She places it carefully in its spot behind the bar, then turns to look at me. "What if Sam hits you?"

I shrug. "I guess I'd feel like I deserved it." I do feel I deserve it. My kid hates me, Karen's disgusted by me, my friends and my work have abandoned me. I'm a loser, but at least I don't have to be a loser coward and that's when I know for sure I'm going to go see Sam and try to make it right, any way I can.

Sam, as in Samantha. As in Samantha Baylor, who worked at the breakfast place on the corner down the street from our white elephant on the beach. I fell into her brown eyes over an order of eggs over easy the first morning we were there. She tolerated my company well enough to let me hang out with the local kids and I played guitar well enough they let me stay. Then my girlfriend from back home in Bryn Mawr, Karen, came to stay with her family for a few weeks and things got very awkward, and Sam made it clear we were going to be friends, just friends.

And we've stayed friends, for almost forty years. I just hope to God I haven't fucked that up, too.

June's sigh brings me back to the bar. "I'm worried about you, Danny Parker. You got this thing about penance, which is fine, but then what? After you let your friend beat the shit out of you? What are you planning then?"

It's my turn to pause. Finally I shake my head. "I guess I don't know."

June takes a deep breath and puts her towel down on the bar. She reaches for another clean glass and pours herself a shot of whiskey, the one she pours every night when she's ready to declare her work done for the day. "I'll tell you what I think you should do," she says, as she raises her glass to me, then swallows.

"What's that?" I watch the liquid move down her throat. The low-lights above the back bar give a honied gloss to her hair and soften the lines on her face. For the first time in a long time, I'm getting some very clear ideas about what I could do, if June will agree. I remember how much I like the taste of whiskey on a willing woman's mouth.

She puts the glass down and covers my hand with hers. "After you find your friend and say you're sorry, go find Southside Johnny. And show him those songs you only talk about when you're too drunk to know what you're saying."

"Okay," I say, just to be nice. I've taken a look at the songs and they're pieces of adolescent crap. I haven't thought about writing a song in so long I don't think I really ever knew how. But I don't have to tell June that. I weave my fingers with hers. I'm reluctant to do this, because of our business relationship, but she looks so round in all the right places. "But before I do either one of those things, could I maybe take you to bed?"

"Aw, Danny," she answers with a sigh. "I thought you'd never ask."

June makes me feel better than I have in a long time. I think I return the favor, because the next morning, she asks me when I'm coming back. I hesitate long enough that she answers for me. "It's okay if you don't, you know...your tab's all clear. You just have to let me know where to send the checks."

I kiss the back of her hand and hold it against my cheek before I shake my head. "I just don't know, Junie-tunes. But I'll be sure to stay in touch, and I'll let you know where I go."

"Fair enough," she says.

Before I leave June's parking lot, just before I turn the key in the ignition, I can't help take another look at the photograph in the bright morning sun. Is it a trick of the morning light, or does my image in the picture possibly look slightly older than it did before?

As luck, or coincidence or fate would have it, Southside and the Jukes are playing at a place on the way to Ocean City, which is where Sam's been living ever since her husband died in a car accident a few years ago. By some miracle there's a seat left, a single seat, just a few rows from the stage.

On the way, driving, I have a lot of time to think. I put on Southside's *I Don't Want To Go Home* CD and let the music carry me back to that first summer my family spent at the Jersey shore, when I was seventeen and knew for certain three things: I desperately wanted to write songs and play guitar in a band – a working band who played real gigs even for miniscule amounts of money if they would only agree to play my songs - and I desperately wanted Sam, who made it very clear that she had no interest in being a summer fling.

But we stayed friends, through the winter, through the spring, through the following summer, and then all through the years Sam stayed in Ocean City, and I practiced my fingers off every minute I wasn't doing whatever it was my parents expected me to do, or writing songs, which was what I really wanted to do.

I was getting ready to graduate, applying to business schools, which is what my parents, Karen and Karen's parents all wanted, when Sam called. The Jukes were looking for a guitar player, she said and a guitar player who could write songs would be a plus.

I remember how ecstatic I was just for the chance.

So I went.

Sam turned out to be dating the drummer. That unsettled me more than I could articulate, even to myself. All I knew was that for some reason, knowing that he was Sam's boyfriend made me want to punch the guy.

And then, just before I had the chance to show off how well I played, just before I could wow them all with every trick and every riff and every bit of honky-tonk finger-picking flash I knew, I got a call from Karen.

Who told me she was late, with that no uncertain meaning.

I remember when Sam took the picture and being angry about how the flash went off in my eyes. It gave me a focus, though, something to hinge my emotions on, and I did the best I could.

I remember when she sent it to me, right after I got the call from Johnny.

His gravelly voice was the last one I expected to hear. "I don't usually like guitar players," he began. "But for a Philly kid, you fit in pretty well. And you play so good, I guess I won't mind if you get all the girls." Then he invited me to play again – at a gig the Jukes were playing at some hole in the wall bar in Rehobeth. But that was after my fate had been sealed, my decisions made.

Karen and I were getting married and I would not be joining a band.

I haven't touched my guitar for more than a few minutes at a time for longer than I can remember. I haven't tried to write a song in even longer.

I get to the show just a few minutes before it's supposed to start. Just before I go inside, I can't help taking another look at the picture. I hope I can get Johnny's attention long enough to ask him to sign it. Showing him the songs… well, that's another story.

I take an even closer look before I put it back inside its envelope. I could swear my hair in the picture is getting grayer. I could swear my hair in the rearview mirror is getting darker.

The old wooden rafters are ringing and the heavy air is pungent with sweat and linseed oil. More than three hundred bodies have packed themselves into the this old music hall to hear Southside Johnny and the Asbury Jukes, and every single one of them, it seems, are yelling and clapping their appreciation as the horns come screaming to a triumphant close.

Except for Johnny, not one of the band looks familiar. Sam stopped dating the drummer a long time ago.

The pounding of the floorboards beneath my feet matches the pounding that started about an hour ago in my head. It seems there's something different about the music tonight, something that's going beyond the more typical connections that form between audience and band, something that feels like the music is trying to drive itself into and through me, all the way to my marrow.

I close my eyes and I am back at the shore, powdery sand beneath my feet, hot sunlight on my face, the scents of salt water taffy and caramel corn buttering the air, too young to understand the possibilities, too young to realize the consequences of what I was throwing away.

The applause dies down as Johnny waves his microphone. "You're great, you're great, thank you," he says, over and over. "We don't ever want the music to stop, do we?"

"No!" roars the crowd, and I join in. My eye is caught by a figure haunting the edges of the stage, darting in and out of the wings. It's a roadie, and he steps into the spotlights to exchange instruments with the guitar player. Even from this distance, I recognize him…he was there that afternoon long ago. I don't remember his name, but I know he was there. The pony tail hanging down his back is even longer than it was then. I decide it's the distance and the effects of the lights that make it seem he hasn't aged a day.

Johnny launches into a powerfully plaintive version of "Just Walk Away, Renee."

I walked away, I think. I walked away from the music, from my life, from the thing that formed the foundation of my soul. I let Karen being late stop me cold, I think. We could've had our son, I think. But maybe I should not have drank the whole punch bowl of Kool-Aid, maybe I shouldn't have so completely thrown my music away.

I stare at the band as they join in, rocking the sound so that the entire building rings, knowing one thing for sure. Whatever I should've, or could've done – or not, it's too late now.

All around me, people are standing, bodies swaying in time to the beat, singing along. Women have their heads on their partners' shoulders, men have their arms around their girls' waists. I stare at the guitar player on stage. I played in a few bands, and I remember how, when I was standing in a similar place, I felt that I was in the place I was supposed to be.

But I walked away from it all, and for thirty years, woke up every morning in a suit and tie that felt like a ball and chain around my neck.

If only there were some way to get those chances – and those years - back.

The song comes to an end with a mournful saxophone flourish and the crowd around me bursts into applause. I'm starting to regret bringing the photograph in with me. It's awkward and getting in the way. I tuck it under my arm in order to clap, and I feel the picture somehow work itself out of the envelope. I pull it out to make sure it's not creased, and glimpse the image of my face.

There's no doubt at all, I think, as I stop cold in the middle of the cheering audience. The face that's looking back at me is the face of a middle-aged man. I spin around on my heel, stumbling a little, so that a few people look at me with disgust as they step out of my way.

The crowd is still applauding and fortunately there's no one else in the men's room. I stare at myself in the tiny oblong above the row of tiny sinks. Then I pull the picture out, and hold it up beside the mirror.

The man in the photograph looks like he's at least fifty ... or more.

The man in the mirror looks no more than twenty-five, if that.

And for the first time in a very long time, the words I'm thinking as I stare at myself sound like they could be the lines of a song.

I forget about asking Johnny to sign the photograph. I don't even stay for the encore. I get into my car and drive to Sam's town. I find a Motel-Six and decide to check in, hoping to spend a few hours scribbling down the words that seem intent on eating their way out of my head.

Or I try to check in, because when the clerk asks for ID, I pull out my driver's license.

But the face in the driver's license doesn't match mine any more.

He throws me out, with an admonishment to get a better fake ID, rather than trying to steal my father's.

That freaks me out.

By this time it's after two AM, the bars are closed and the streets are empty. If a cop stops me – with my out of state plates and no identifiable form of ID - I'm screwed.

Without a clear thought about where to go, I head toward the ocean, and find a little parking lot across the street from a beach where Sam and I and the rest of the kids used to play volleyball. There are a few city trucks parked at one end, and I ease my car between two of them.

I spend the rest of the night in the back seat, words pouring through my fingers and onto the Dunkin Donut napkins I find stashed in the glove box.

By the time the sun comes up, I have the beginnings of what's starting to sound like a song.

What if this is Purgatory
This is where you do your time
And your choices with your chances
Define where you draw the lines
Between Hell and Purgatory
Between Purgatory and Paradise
Because, baby, there's a heaven;
And I'm heading there tonight;
I know that there's a heaven –
Will you come with me tonight?

We all got our stories
We all got our lines
Everybody gets their chances
Everybody does their time
And making it or breaking it
Has nothing to do with sin
It's how well you live the story
Of the life you're walking in

And I know that there's a heaven
Because I'm heading there tonight
I know that's there's a heaven
Will you come with me, girl, tonight?

I feel the ghost of a melody trying to peek through the lines, like the thin disk of the red sun that's coming up behind the low-lying clouds over the water.

The air that engulfs me when I get out to stretch my legs is moist and smells like salt. From where I'm standing, I can only glimpse the beach beyond the dunes, but I can hear the rhythm of the surf washing over the sand.

I feel gritty and tired and raw. My fingers are cramped, my wrist is numb. I haven't written so much by hand in a long time, and I am exhausted, but elated.

I tuck the napkins carefully back in the glove box and follow the scent and the sound of the ocean to the beach.

Maybe when I get back in the car, and look in the mirror, I'll be changed back into my old self. Maybe, like Cinderella, the magic only lasted the night. Maybe the photograph really didn't change – maybe it was just a trick of the light in the men's room. Maybe I'm just at the end of my rope.

In the growing grayish light, I look down at my hands. They are fit and strong and brown, a young man's hands, with callouses on the tips just the way there used to be, back when I played my guitar all the time.

I stare at the callouses, chills going up my arms and down my back. I feel a little dizzy, a little faint. I don't understand what's happened to me, but I'm starting to think it could be permanent – and real.

I look up and down. Nothing moves but the gulls taking it in turn to rise from their nests between the rocks, then wheel and shriek above the water. A wave, bigger than the others, rushes nearly to my feet. It feels like an invitation. The beach is deserted and the ocean is beckoning.

I strip down inside the lifeguard stand, and run into the water.

The late-September ocean is warm, but the morning air raises immediate goose bumps all over. I don't care. I dive into the oncoming froth, and surface to see the edge of the sun balancing on the horizon, long rays of red light spreading like ribbons of blood across the gray-green water.

I'm dreading talking to Sam. I get out, feeling cleaner but no less afraid. I dry off as best I can with my t-shirt, but I can't help getting sand in all the wrong crevices.

Before I go looking for coffee, I decide to look for Sam's house. A few grains of sand have lodged themselves in my underwear. I have to find a men's room, I think, as I settle myself as comfortably as possible in the driver's seat.

But first I want to make sure I know where I'm going.

Her street's on the other side of town, the second block back from the bay. As I pull up to the little gray bungalow nestled between two larger houses, I'm surprised to see a For Sale sign. Then I remember why I've come in the first place.

Jesus, I think. She's been forced to sell her house. I will be lucky if she doesn't beat me up. The Sam I remember was always a feisty little thing.

Before I can drive away, the front door opens, and a small woman who can only be Sam steps out onto the small porch that's really more of a stoop. In the pearly light, her hair's a darker shade of brown, but she's just as slim and light on her feet as I remember.

I try to slink down behind the wheel before she notices me, but she's too quick as she bends to pick up her paper. She sees me as she gets up. Her robe is the same peachy pink as the sky. She pulls it closer together as she peers hard in my direction.

I don't want to make her afraid. Before she gets too nervous, I grab my envelope with the photograph, so I can prove who I am, and get out. "Sam?" I shut the door gently so I don't sound threatening, and slowly make my way around the car. There's no doubt it's Sam...but a Sam who looks as if she hasn't aged a day in thirty years. Or more. "Sam, is that you? It's me... Danny."

Her hand flies to her mouth. "Oh my God, Danny," she says. "Holy shit." She comes down the three or four steps to the cement walkway. "You look... you look... you look like... like the you I remember." The paper falls to the ground as she presses both her hands to her cheeks, and her eyes fill up with tears.

I can't quite believe her reaction. She doesn't look angry. She doesn't sound angry. She looks surprised and even happy to see me. Whatever's happened to me, I see that the same thing's happened to her, and that makes me feel better, much better, despite the sand that's starting to itch. "So do you."

"Yeah," she says, with a sniff and a little laugh. "Yeah, it's pretty un-believable, isn't it? I got to tell you...I'm not quite sure what to make of it."

"What – uh – what have you told people?"

"Told people? I haven't seen any people to tell. I just woke up like this...about twenty minutes ago. I went to bed, maybe not looking exact-ly like the Crypt-keeper, but getting close. And I wake up looking better than I can ever remember looking – or maybe it's because I appreciate it more now." She takes a couple more steps in my direction, and beckons. "Why don't you come inside? Car's fine parked on the street – they don't clean these backstreets after Labor Day any more. You look like you could use a cup of coffee – or six. And you know...I have something for you. You're not going to believe this... but... well, I guess maybe both of us can believe anything, now, right?"

I am too astonished to move. "But, Sam, wait...aren't you angry with me? The last time we talked...I told you to buy as much of my so-called wonder stock as you could. Didn't you lose it all when the news came out about the CFO? Isn't that why you have to sell the house?"

"No," says Sam. "Who says I *have* to sell the house?" She shakes her head and grins. Her short haircut makes her look more like a pixie than ever. "I'm selling the house because I want to sell the house, Dan. I'm going on the road. Not sure where, not sure how long I'll be gone." She picks up my hand and tugs me toward the porch. "Come on, you have to see this...what I've got for you...You'll be amazed, really."

"But..." I can't imagine being more amazed again than I am right now. Sam's not angry. In a dark recess of my heart, something I thought long dead begins to sing. "You have to tell me." I pause at the bottom of the peeling painted steps. "That's why I'm here. I'm here to apologize to you, to say I'm sorry for –"

"For what?" She turns on the top step in one of her quicksilver moves. "Don't you remember telling me, Danny, that bulls make money, bears make money, but pigs get slaughtered?"

Of course I remember telling her that. I told everyone that. It was my favorite Wall Street saying, especially in the beginning.

She tugs on my hand, pulling me, still unbelieving, up the steps. "When the stock went over a hundred dollars a share, I remembered how you said that pigs get slaughtered, and I started feeling like a pig. So I decided to sell it...which, as it happened, was right before the bad news came out. I got the best possible price, I think, or close enough that I don't care."

I stumble over the threshold, as Sam leads me into a house that's decorated in what Karen used to dismiss with a sneer as "grandma's attic." In the kitchen, she points out the chair most likely to hold my weight. I put the envelope on the table and sit. It wobbles a bit, but seems sturdy enough. "So... so you're not destitute? You're not going to starve because I made a terrible call?"

"Not in the least." She pats my shoulder, smiles reassuringly, then busies herself with coffee, while I sit, still shocked. As the fragrance starts to perfume the kitchen, she nods at my envelope. "What's in there?"

I fumble with the edge. "It's a picture... one of those photographs you took... of me and Southside, the day I auditioned. You remember?"

"I sure do," she says. She opens a drawer and removes a framed photograph. She places it in front of me. "Someone else took this one. I think it must've been Paulie."

The photograph in the simple black frame is clearly from the same roll, but taken after we've been playing a while and the band is taking a break. I'm looking much more relaxed, Johnny is looking drenched. The angle of the lens now includes the drums, where Sam's mugging for the camera...a Sam whose image is at least a generation older than the girl sitting before me now. She gasps, softly, and I look up. She leans over my shoulder, and I feel the pressure of her breasts against my back.

"Oh, my God," she says, tapping on the glass with a fingertip. "Oh, my God. Look at this. I didn't notice this...didn't even think to look at this, until just now because you showed up...my God, look at me. Look at this...it's like I've changed places with the girl I used to be."

I slide my photograph out from its envelope. "Look," I reply. "See? It's happened to me, too." Her hands are shaking as she picks the photo up, examining it.

I look at hers more closely. The photo is autographed, I realize, signed by Southside in two places. Under her face, Johnny has written "Long time no C." Under mine, he's written "Better late than never." I look up at Sam. The morning light is tender on her twenty-year old face. "When did you get this signed?"

She hesitates, then shrugs. "Just a few weeks ago. I found it... when I was cleaning out some stuff, getting this place ready to sell. See, the thing is, Danny..." She sinks down opposite onto a chair that emits a long protesting squeak. "I knew you were probably in trouble. I wanted to do something – anything – but, I didn't know what. I tried calling your office a few weeks after it happened, but they said you were gone. I tried calling your house but got Karen who launched into such a tirade against you I just hung up. I only had your work email. Every time I called your cellphone, you never picked up and your voice mail was full. I wanted to thank you... but... I didn't know how to reach you."

I want to take her in my arms and kiss her but I let her keep talking.

"So one day, as I was cleaning up, getting the house ready to sell, I found this photograph. And I remembered that day...how great you played, how much everyone liked you, how I really thought this was going to be your chance. And then how it all came crashing down...just the way it just had. But I was getting a second chance, to do all the stuff I wanted to do... I just wanted you to know how grateful I am and if there was anything I could do to help you, but ...like I said, I didn't know how to get in touch with you. So then I got the idea that someone had to be forwarding your mail. So I looked up where the band was playing, and found a show not too far from here, and took the picture. And during the show, while he was singing that part where everyone joins in and sings 'oooh it'll be all right?' Well, just then I made a little wish that it really would be all right, for both of us, and that you would get the same kind of second chance that you helped me get."

She takes a deep breath and wraps her hands around her mug, to keep them from shaking, I think. "So here's where it gets a little weird. After the show, I was standing in line, waiting for a chance to ask Johnny to sign the photograph, when one of his roadies – this guy who's been with the band for ages – he was even there when you auditioned, but I don't know if you'd remember him –"

"The one with long pony tail?"

"Yeah," says Sam. "You know who I mean?"

"I saw Johnny and the Jukes last night. I noticed that guy in the background...and I did remember him. That pony tail is just the same. He's got to be ten years older than we are and he looks great, for someone his age. Something's sure keeping him young. You know his name?"

Sam nods. "Yeah...his name's George. So anyway, I'm waiting in line, waiting for my turn, and George comes up to me. I recognized him immediately – mostly because – like you said - he doesn't look much older than he did then. He was such a great roadie, but there was always something a little strange about him. He was always there in the right place or time with the exactly what the guys needed. Paulie said it was uncanny sometimes, 'cause it was like he would just know and show up before you could even ask for it – whatever it was.

"But anyway, George comes up to me and we hug and kiss, and he asks about Paulie. He asks about me. And then he hands me this guitar pick – with your picture on it. He said you'd dropped it that day at the audition, and he found it in someone's gig bag at that show they asked you to play in Delaware, and that he always meant to give it back." She leans forward. "He said to tell you you'd played great – that everyone was really disappointed you never came back. Danny, it was like he *knew* I'd be seeing you. And that's when I knew – just knew in a way I can't explain it – that I didn't have to send you anything, that you'd be coming to find me."

From the same drawer, she removes a small packet of folded tissue paper. She unwraps the tissue, and places a cream-colored guitar pick with a tiny photograph imprinted on it in front of me. My photograph. From my high school year book. Just like the others I found in the file with this photograph and my songs.

I pick it up and it's warm, like I only just put it down. I can't begin to understand how this has happened, but I guess I have to accept that it has. It's going to complicate my life in a million different ways that I probably haven't even begun to imagine but I have a feeling it's all going to work out. I turn the little piece of ivory plastic between my fingers. That makes the words that I wrote last night come back to me, this time to a beat. *What if this is Pur-ga-to-ry...* There's a melody hiding in there, too, and a key that feels like it wants to be B flat.

Sam touches my arm before I start to hum. "You thinking about a song?"

That she guesses this startles me. I place the pick on the table, next to the photograph, as she puts two cups of steaming coffee on the checkered oilskin tablecloth that looks like it could've come from her grandmother's attic. "How did you know?"

"Because that's what you used to do when you were thinking about a song. You'd play with a pick the way you were doing, and stare into space. And you'd have this look on your face like you did just now, and whenever you looked that way, I knew you were thinking about a song."

I smile that she remembers this. This is the first morning in a long time I've been so happy. I touch Southside's scrawl under my image. "Why did you have him write this?"

"I didn't," she replies. "He just wrote that. Without my saying a thing."

"Wow," I say, because there really isn't anything else I can think to say.

"Drink your coffee before it gets cold," she says. "And let's talk about if you'd like to come with me and if so, where you think we ought to go?"

"Where do you think we should go?" I ask, because I really don't care, as long as I can go with her.

She covers my hand with hers. "I say we go find Southside Johnny and ask him what he meant."

The End

Raising Jerry Garcia
(with Don Goodman)

Celebrity Supernatural #3

I

When Bernadette calls to tell me that Stevie Garracino is missing … as in gone … as in not seen for nearly twenty four hours … I'm too busy to even hear the phone ring. The day before, the mother of all summer storms hit our little town on the South Jersey shore, knocking out all the power, leaving streaming streets and debris-blocked avenues.

In its aftermath, the August weather has turned predictably gorgeous – if you're one of the tourists still stranded here or the National Guard that's come to dig us out, that is.

If you're running a flower shop on the first floor of your house as a cover for the illegal pot-growing operation on the third floor, not so much. I'm not just out of business until the power comes back on. I have a much bigger problem.

It's two o'clock in the afternoon and Bob, Debby and I have just finished watering all the plants. Without the ventilation and watering systems operating, not only is the entire crop threatened, but we're in jeopardy of having our whole business come tumbling down around us. Without the carbon filters syphoning the air, in the August heat, even with every one of the windows in the entire twenty-seven room house open, the place is going to reek like a marijuana farm in no more than a day or two.

Maybe I'm paranoid, but I'm sure I'm starting to smell it in the store, two floors below. With the house situated on a busy side street, it's just a matter of time before passersby smell it too.

"I could try hooking up a couple fans to a couple car batteries," offers Bob dubiously. His threadbare khaki shorts and faded Grateful Dead t-shirt belie the fact he's really an accountant in his early 40's whose been cooking the books for the business since we started growing almost ten years ago. But long before all that, in his teens, Bob worked for his dad, who was an electrician.

He's standing at the point in the hallway where you can see into most of the third floor bedrooms. What you can see from that vantage point are about fifty of the most pungent plants we've ever grown, all in the early stages of budding.

I'm further down the hall, feeling a breeze beginning to stir off the ocean. "Don't be silly. That's not going to solve the problem."

Behind Bob, Debby comes out of the bathroom with the last of the watering cans. I see Debby cock her head toward the stairs that lead down to my second floor apartment. "Hey," she says, tapping Bob. "Do you hear the phone?"

"You know, Mary Beth," Bob's saying. "I really think I could get something rigged."

"Bob, it's not blowing the air around that's the issue...it's the smell."

"I'm sure I hear the phone...I think I'll go grab it." Debby practically scampers down the steps. Not that I blame her. The fact that Bob's dad died when he accidentally electrocuted himself rewiring a house doesn't inspire anyone's confidence in Bob's electrical prowess and has a lot to do with why Bob's an accountant.

"Hey," Bob says. "Does that mean the power's back on?"

"No," I shake my head sadly as I walk back down the long hallway. "It's a real old-fashioned landline... the phone itself is wired into the house. It'll work come hell or high water... in fact, it has."

"Hey, you guys up there?"

From far below, I hear Debby. I lean down and shout back, "What's up?"

"It's Bernadette... on the phone... she's at Stevie's house, with his mom." Debby's voice gets louder. She peers up at us from the bottom of the steps. "Have either of you seen Stevie? Since, like, before the storm?"

We troop downstairs to my kitchen. We're exhausted and dirty, and not just from tending the plants. The whole town's a mess, the beach blocks hit especially hard. It could be days before the power comes back on.

We sink into the old wooden chairs and rip into beers. "What's this about Stevie gone missing?" asks Bob through a belch.

"Classy," chides Debby. "Bernie's on her way over. Mrs. G is really upset."

"Bernie's going to be upset if you call her that." I say to Debby. There's always been the teensiest edge of rivalry between the two of them. Debby has a thing for Bob. Bob has a thing for Bernadette. Debby's a ringletted blonde earth mother, who may have gained a few pounds over the years but mostly in all the right places. And Bernadette... well, my first impression of Bernadette when I met her nearly twenty years ago was that she was simply too beautiful to be flesh and blood.

As if on cue, the back door swings open and Bernadette steps over the threshold, looking as fresh as a tampon commercial compared to the rest of us. It helps, of course, that she lives offshore, and her town wasn't hit anywhere near as badly as our little barrier island.

She begins to remove her rain-boots, then glances across the linoleum floor. Sand is everywhere – you can't walk outside without picking up wet sand and tracking it anywhere you go. She straightens, and accepts a beer. But she doesn't drink it, and she isn't smiling. She doesn't even seem to care that the business is in jeopardy. "Mrs. G's completely terrified," Bernadette says, before any of us can say anything much more than hello. "Have you heard from him? Seen him?"

"Bernie," says Debby, pulling out a chair. "Come on, sit down. You mean Stevie just up and left his 80 year old mother in the middle of a storm? That hardly makes sense."

"Why do you think I'm so freaked out," Bernadette paces to the window, stares out across the street as if Stevie might be skulking in the debris piled against the water-logged cars. "A neighbor's been with her since she realized he's been gone, thank God. She says she's been calling over here... why haven't you answered the phone?"

"Because I've been busy tending the crop." Sometimes Bernadette forgets she was our friend long before she thought about law school. But I understand why she's so upset. Stevie and his mother may not always get along in the warmest and fuzziest of ways, but I'm having a hard time believing Stevie would leave in the middle of a storm. He hated to get wet.

"Bernie, maybe it's some Navy thing," says Bob. "They have the Army Corps of Engineers here...maybe Stevie got called up?"

"Stevie left the Navy hating it," Bernadette answers, the skin around her eyes and mouth as taut as a hunted doe's. "Five years ago." She must be really upset, I realize. She didn't tell either Bob or Debby not to call her Bernie. "He'd never go back."

"Well," Bob says, caressing the edges of his beer bottle like a woman's lips. Bob can't keep his eyes off Bernadette. Sometimes I wish Bob and Bernadette would just give into the thing they have, and get it over with. But I also know that would change all the dynamics of what we have going on between the five of us, and I'm not in any hurry to change that. "He hasn't officially worked for anyone for over five years. But that's not to say he's not working... you really think he's living off Mrs. G?"

"Mrs. G wants to call the police," Bernadette says, tapping her foot.

"Oh, my God," say Debby and I together.

"No… no," continues Debby, because I'm too stunned by the realization that as Stevie's closest friend, if he really has disappeared, I'm one of the first people they will question, and this is one of the first places the police will come. "We're not…we're not, like, secure." Debby glances at Bob then back to me. "Right, guys?"

"Well, yeah." I say. Without ventilation filters, the smell wafting downstairs is about to get incredibly intense. I'm as worried about Stevie as Bernadette… more probably, but the last thing we need is to jeopardize the cottage industry the five of us have built. We help people, people with real problems from cancer to anxiety disorders. And maybe we did start growing pot for ourselves, but that doesn't make our mission any less noble. Or us, any less criminal. But the idea Stevie's met with some kind of foul play isn't what worries me.

That he's gone and done something batshit crazy does. "I need… we need… a least a couple days… especially if the power stays off. The longer it does… the stronger the plants are going to smell. The whole crop's about to bud. We can't… we can't let police come here, not even to the store now."

"Why do you think I came rushing over here as fast as I could? Did you know they're thinking of closing the bridges after five pm? You can't believe what I had to go through to get here." Bernadette stalks back across the room.

"So you haven't seen him either, since the storm?" Bernadette asks in her lawyer voice.

I rack my brain, trying to remember, wanting to be sure. "No," I say finally. "And to be honest, I've been so worried about the plants, I haven't given much thought to anyone or anything else." When I haven't been up on the third floor dealing with the illegal weed, I've been down in the garage-turned-greenhouse dealing with the legal plants we grow as a cover.

Stevie has a condition called synesthesia, which means his senses are all tangled up in his brain. But that's not the least of it. Stevie's condition manifests in the kind of genius that borders on craziness – or laziness, as his mother calls it. Which, I guess, to be fair, is what it could be, until you understand it.

And I didn't, not for a very long time, until one night just a few months ago when Stevie blew a hole in my mind big enough for the entire Grateful Dead to come marching through. So it's not just the idea of calling the police and having the jail door slam on the business that disturbs me. It's knowing that the police might not be capable of doing anything to find Stevie that really worries me.

"How long has it been since you heard from him?" Bernadette asks. "Any of you?"

"A couple days before the storm," replies Debby. "No, I think it was actually the day before…he called me at work…he was all excited about getting together as soon as we could … he said he had a breakthrough."

"Yeah," says Bob. "Me, too. I think I talked to him Monday… he says he'd made a major breakthrough…something he couldn't wait to share."

"So you talked to him Monday, you talked to him Tuesday… the storm hit Wednesday… Mary Beth, what about you?"

There was something in the way Bernadette's asking that makes me feel like I'm 17 and caught by the principal. "I…I talked to him both days." I glance around the room. Everyone knows Stevie and I have a… thing. It's a thing and not a relationship because Mrs. G is right about one thing: Stevie would rather spend time in his attic than just about anywhere else. "Bernadette, what're you getting at?"

"You know this is a bad time of year for Stevie," hisses Bernadette. In a blink, she turns from prosecuting attorney into worried friend. "The storm hit August ninth. You know what that means."

Puzzled, I shake my head, look at Bob, then Debby.

Bob clears his throat and puts his empty beer bottle down on the sticky oilcloth. "It's been three years since Jerry died."

It has to be just a coincidence that the storm happened on the day Jerry died. Stevie can't possibly have had anything to do with the storm. Then I think about all I know about Stevie. "I think we should go talk to Mrs. G."

Bernadette hands me her untouched beer. "I think that's a really good idea."

II

We clean up as best we can because according to Mrs. G, cleanliness is next to Godliness and she won't be shy about telling us if we smell like pot. Bob suggests we stop at the beach on the way to Mrs. G's for a quick dip in the warm August ocean – better to be salty than sweaty. We must smell pretty ripe, because Bernadette agrees, even though Mrs. G lives back by the bay, the whole opposite direction.

We decide to take two cars. "Will you come with me?" Bernadette asks me.

"Sure," I answer. I can see how upset she is. Which is odd, because I would've said, if anyone asked me, that of the five of us, the pair who are the least close is Bernadette and Stevie.

I can see she's near tears as she puts the car in gear and heads toward the ocean. "Bernadette," I say gently. "What's up? I know it's awful that Stevie's missing, but you seem to be upset about more than that. When was the last time you talked to Stevie?"

"Two weeks ago," she says, shaking her head. "And I think it's my fault that he's…that he's gone."

"What are you talking about, honey? How could you be responsible for him going anywhere?"

"Last time we all got together – two weeks ago – our quarterly business meeting? Remember I gave him a ride home? I…I asked him what he thought he was doing with his life. I think…I know he took it badly." The car rolls to a gentle stop at a red light.

Straight ahead, I should be able to see an unobstructed view of the boardwalk at the end of the street. But what I see instead looks like some sort of police barricade, with saw horses draped with yellow tape. "He got upset?"

"He asked me when I was going to get it over with and fuck Bob."

My eyebrows fly up. "I guess he got upset." On some level both are fair questions. Bernadette and Bob have been eyeing each other for nearly twenty years. And as far as we know, Stevie doesn't do anything more than take care of his mother and the house they live in. The rest of his time is spent in what his mother calls his cave – the attic he's converted into the highest tech sound-proof room I think anyone outside the CIA ever imagined.

"I didn't mean anything by it," she says. The Jeep bounces over driftwood, crunches over piles of sand and shells. "But Stevie's a genius, and all he does is sit in that room of his...Have you noticed he's starting to look...wet?" She looks at me sideways and her voice quivers. "He's not getting enough sunlight... he's turning gray. And, come on, Mary Beth, doesn't it bother you he's not doing something more with his life?"

I stare back at her, not quite sure how to answer. On some level, of course it bothers me that Stevie would rather stare into space in the dark. But the glimpses I've seen of his life don't look like a picnic to me. "You know Stevie's different, Bernadette. His condition... it's easier for him in the dark."

"You mean it's easier for him to stay stoned and listen to music in the dark." Bernadette looks like she's sucked on a lemon. "Who isn't that easier for?"

Ahead of us, Bob's SUV rolls to a stop. A uniformed soldier holding a gun is waving him to the right. He makes the turn, then pulls over to the curb a few yards up. Bernadette follows, and brakes beside him. "They say we can't get any closer to the beach," Bob says through his open window.

"I can't believe how bad it all looks," Debby says, leaning over Bob. "Whole sections of the boardwalk are, like, swept away."

"I think we should just head over to Mrs. G," says Bernadette.

It takes us longer than I expected, because there're so many downed lines and trees and streets still half-covered by water and debris. And on some blocks, it looks like there's a soldier or a cop on every corner.

"Well, that's just great," says Bob, as he gets out of his car. He watches the two uniformed soldiers marching down the block on the opposite side of the street. He waves at them. "Just checking in on an old lady... Nothing to worry about here."

"Stop it, Bob, this isn't Kent State." Bernadette elbows his side. "They're on our side now, remember?"

Bob rolls his eyes. "You let them get an eyeful of Mary Beth's third floor and we'll see what side they're on."

As we file up the porch steps, Debby turns back to look at me. "Mary Beth, are you okay?"

If Bernadette feels guilty, she has no idea how responsible I feel. Because unlike everyone else, I do have an inkling about what Stevie's doing with his time, up in his cave. The last time I saw Stevie Garracino he was higher than a kite and it had nothing to do with the weed we were smoking. It had everything to do with the fact he was sure he'd found a way to bring Jerry Garcia – or at least Jerry's music - back from the dead.

I don't believe anything Bernadette said would cause Stevie to do anything to hurt himself.

But I do believe I didn't take Stevie seriously when he told me what he was doing.

The five of us met in September of 1979 when we went to work for the Social Security Administration. We'd been hired to learn how to code benefit documents. We were part of a class of about thirty-five, which by the end of the first week had divided itself into Jocks & Prom Queens, Normal People and Everyone Else.

The five of us were obviously Everyone Else. We shared at least three things in common: we were all from little towns in South Jersey, we were all recent graduates of institutions of higher learning; and the degrees we possessed from those institutions in things like English (me), French (Deb), Philosophy (Bob and Bernadette) and Music (Stevie) automatically disqualified us from immediately pursuing more lucrative career paths.

And we had all, for reasons various and sundry, attended the Englishtown, NJ concert of the Grateful Dead in 1977.

Of us five, Debby and Stevie were the ones who followed the band around in the summers. Bob had four younger sisters to help his widowed mother raise, and while he might resemble the quintessential Deadhead, Bob's actually the most disciplined of us all. Bernadette's like me – we had boyfriends who were into the band, and it was fun to tag along.

Now the porch door slams shut behind me, bringing me back to the present and the Garracinos' postage-stamp sized living room. Like everything else in town, it smells like sand dunes at low tide. It also smells like sour milk and pee.

Mrs. G is ensconced in her big red chair, dressed, as usual, in one of her pink housecoats. Her crochet bag is on the floor beside her. Her neighbor, Agnes Annarelli, is bending over her with a steaming tea cup as we all troop in. I steel myself for the certain onslaught. Mrs. G might be little, but she's incredibly fierce. "Well, well," she says, "Look who's here at last."

Agnes looks at us, relief obvious. "I'm glad you guys got here before I had to leave. I got to get to work – they switched my shift, and with all this damage, God knows I need the work."

"Don't worry. We'll make sure she's okay." Bob says. He sinks down on the ottoman next to Mrs. G's chair, as Agnes makes a quick escape. "And Stevie... we'll make sure he's okay, too."

"Like the four of you give a rat's ass about an old lady." Mrs G snorts, shifts in her chair, and gestures at Bernadette with the tea cup. "Take this for me, will you? Put it over there... Agnes means well but she's got the brain of a flea."

"I'm sorry I didn't pick up, Mrs. G," I say. "We've been so busy with the plants...it never occurred to me that you and Stevie weren't okay. I can't believe he'd leave you alone in the middle of a storm."

"Don't give me that dumb routine, Mary Beth. He leaves me alone all the time." She nods at the door at the end of the hall that leads to Stevie's lair. "Up there in his attic, what good is he to me? I wouldn't know he was gone but the power went out and I figured he might break his neck coming down those steps in the dark. So I opened the door and shouted upstairs, but he's gone. Gone and left an old lady alone to fend for herself." She looks at all of us in turn, more accusingly than any prosecutor. "What kind of a person does that?"

"Maybe, like, a distracted person?" offers Debby.

"I'll tell you what kind of a person," says Mrs. G. Her white hair resembles an exploding dandelion and her beady blue eyes behind her glasses rake our semicircle once more. "A drugged-out hippie who cares more about music than he cares about his mother. That's what kind of a person."

"Oh, Mrs. G." Bob makes a gesture as if to pat her hand, then seems to think better of it. "That's harsh."

"You want to know what harsh is?" She straightens up, and the hairy little cushion on her lap turns into her Maltese, Harold. "Harsh is leaving me alone with no power. That's harsh."

Bob visibly cringes, then gets to his feet. "And that's the door that goes upstairs, right, Mrs. G?" Bob points down the hall.

"You know it is."

"He couldn't have come downstairs without you seeing him, and there's no other way out of the attic?"

"There's a fire escape door up there. There had to be... couldn't have a space to code without two ways out. And why would Stevie leave me in the middle of all this mess but to deal with some drug... problem? Isn't that what makes the most sense?" She glares at each of us. "I know why you're here. You just don't want me to call the police."

"We're here to make sure you're okay," says Debby, switching from the wing chair to the ottoman.

"Maybe you could get some things together," says Bernadette. "While we go up to the attic and try to figure out if Stevie's left a note."

As we start up the steps, I say, "I know Stevie wouldn't just... just leave. She's difficult, but he wouldn't... he wouldn't...abandon her." Stevie's not like that, I think. He might be everything his mother says he is, but he's kind, gentle. When he remembers you're there. That's the reality of dealing with Stevie... he's so lost inside his own world he forgets about everyone else's.

"Are you sure?" says Bob. "I'd be out of here toot sweet. How the fuck does he put up with that woman?"

"He smokes a lot of pot," replies Debby.

"And spends all his time in the attic," hisses Bernadette, following right behind me. "Do you see this place? Do you smell this place? He's clearly not keeping it up. The question is how does she put up with him? Because really, if he's up in this attic all the time, how well is he really taking care of her?"

Bob looks over his shoulder. "C'mon, Bernie, it's not so bad. It's that Addams Family look that never goes out of style: peeling paint, chipping wallpaper."

Debby snorts. "You mean chipping paint and peeling wallpaper."

Bob steps into the attic. "Wow," he says. "And a lot of ruined equipment."

The smell of the bay hits me like an old fish as we crowd into the space behind Bob. On the opposite side, the fire escape door seems to have gotten stuck wide open at some point during the storm. Water stains the walls and the rugs; equipment and papers are strewn chaotically around the floor.

"If he left a note, good luck finding it," mutters Debby.

"What the fuck is all this?" asks Bob. Despite the damage from the storm, some sort of low level lighting like the kind they have in airplanes, runs all around the perimeter, still giving off a weird bluish glow. It reflects off the metal edges of the equipment, of the desks, illuminating the debris. And on the sloping ceiling, equations written in glow-in-the-dark markers shimmer in the weird light.

"Einstein meets the Grateful Dead," I say.

"Smells more like Fulton Fish Market meets the Grateful Dead," Bernadette says with a disdainful sniff, hesitating to take more than a step or two. The floor's covered with rainbow colored bits of post-it paper, cords and electrical wires of all thicknesses and colors, some bundled together, others tangling into a trap calculated to break the ankles of the unwary, all connected to the mountains of amplifiers and motherboards and speakers and screens banked around room.

"What the fuck is all this?" says Bob again, stepping bravely over the coils of wires, where above and around Stevie's desk, a wall of speakers absorbs the light like a black hole.

"I don't think we should touch anything," I say. "This is his project. This is what he does."

"His project, huh?" Bob stops short as he reaches the desk, me right behind him. Four sets of red numbers are blinking on and off. "And if the power's out, why are they still on?"

"I imagine he has backup batteries," I answer. "Stevie's backups have backups."

"He was really into some weird shit, wasn't he?" says Bernadette, still hanging back.

It hits me then, with her use of the past tense, that she really does believe the absolute worst. "You really do think he's dead, don't you?"

With that, Bernadette bounds across the floor, heedless of the cables. "Could you keep your voice down, Mary Beth? And don't you?"

"Oh, c'mon, Bernie." Bob shakes his head. "We always knew Stevie was into weird shit, even before the Navy. It's just...." He looks at the equipment, computers, screens and amplifiers, and keyboards, both the typing and musical kind. "I clearly had no idea how fucking weird." He points to the cassette tape rack that stretches across one entire wall. The storm has toppled at least half of them onto the floor, but there's still thousands, labelled in Stevie's neat block letters stacked on the rack. "Do you see this... did you know he has all these, Mary Beth? These are like... what... every freaking thing the Dead ever did? Jesus, that's exactly what this is." He starts sorting through the tapes, picking up one, then another.

But he very quickly stops. "Holy God, no, it's more than that, isn't it?" He looks at me, almost accusingly, like I've been holding out on him, too. "This is every version, every bootleg, of everything the Dead ever did." He shakes his head, swears more under his breath. "I can't believe he's been fucking holding out on me like this."

"Do you know what he's doing up here, Mary Beth?" asks Debby. "Do you know what his project's about?"

I shrug. It never occurred to me to question or judge what it is exactly Stevie does up here, alone, in the dark, with his colors and his music and his math. He's the primary caregiver for his mother and I've seen caregiving kill more than one spouse, parent or child. If Stevie's way of relaxing diverted him down some lurid paths... well, I'm not sure I could spend five minutes with the harpy in the living room.

"Damn it, Mary Beth," says Bernadette.

"Hey now," says Bob, looking up from his knees. "You don't have to go all prosecuting attorney, Bernie. Mary Beth, there's nothing you're not telling us, is there?"

I shake my head. "I've got no idea where Stevie is, or where he could be, or where he might've gone. I take a deep breath, steeling myself for scrutiny turning to scorn. "I know what he's been doing... what he's been trying to do." I pause. Damn it, Stevie, I think. This really isn't supposed to be my job. I hope that twenty years of friendship will be enough to keep them from immediately calling the men in white coats. "He was trying to bring back Jerry Garcia."

There's a long, long silence, or at least it feels like a long silence. Bob and Bernadette and Debby all exchange glances at each other, then all look at me.

"Seriously?" Bernadette says.

"Wasn't Jerry cremated?" asks Bob.

"Yeah," says Debby. "Like, just exactly how was he planning on doing that?"

I take another deep breath, and try not to swear at Stevie, wherever he might be. Any explanation I can stumble through is bound to sound lame. And crazy. "Not Jerry, himself, obviously... we're not talking Night of the Living Dead. He wanted to bring back Jerry's music, to prove to himself that the music really does go on forever. But don't ask me how."

I gesture to the banks of equipment, the sound systems, the computers, the equations on the ceilings and the ruined rainbow of post-it notes. "All I know, it involved all this." And my birthday present, I want to say. But I really don't know how to explain that, so I decide not to say anything about it. Not just yet.

Bernadette clears her throat, then points to the four sets of red numbers that continue to flash over Stevie's desk. "You have any idea what those are?"

11:23:58. 13:21:34. 05:05:08. 09:01:44.

I shake my head, shrug. "I don't know...anyone?"

"Dates?" says Bernadette. "November 23, 1958?"

Bob looks up, then at the tapes. "Maybe the numbers correlate to concerts? Or songs... songs in certain concerts?"

I venture a guess. "Maybe it's the time. 11:23 and 58 seconds. The thirteen is one in the afternoon. What do you think?" I look around the attic. "Well?"

Everyone shrugs. "I'll buy that," Debby says. She picks up a scrap of paper off the floor and writes them down. "Just in case."

"Just in case what?" Bernadette says impatiently.

Without warning, Mrs. G shouts upstairs, "Yoohoo, Bernadette? Mary Beth? Anyone up there? There's a young man here who says we have to leave. There's a gas line leak."

Debby holds up the paper. "See? Just in case we have to leave." She tucks it in her pocket, then dashes down the steps. "I'm coming, Mrs. G."

Bernadette actually stamps her foot. "Just as we're about to figure something out? Now, isn't that just fucking great."

"Bernie," says Bob, as he uncoils himself from the floor, and starts stuffing tapes in his pockets, "did I just hear you say fucking?"

III

We bundle Mrs. G and the dog into Bernadette's Jeep. "I think I should take Mrs. G and Harold home with me," she announces, when we roll up to the water-covered curb in front of my first floor florist shop. "What if there's a gas leak in this block? I'm offshore.... We didn't get anything close to the damage you did."

One look at Mrs. G, and the depth of the water still puddled on the sidewalk, and I can't agree fast enough. I wave them goodbye as Bob and Debby pull up. "No Mrs. G?" he says. "Thank God."

"No Bernadette either, thank God," I say, watching the red tail lights disappear around the block. Thank God she's upset enough to take Mrs. G off our hands.

"Mary Beth," Debby says, gently tapping my arm. "Mary Beth, is there any more we need to do? Like, with the plants?"

I meet her eyes. The sun's going down, it's getting dark. "The breeze's picked up...hopefully that's going to help. Let's hose off, roll a fatty and barbecue something from the freezer before it all goes bad."

"You really don't mind if we both stay the night?"

"Of course not," I reply. "I need you here to help me protect the crop."

We find candles and flashlights, and take turns hosing ourselves off in the shower. Bob fires up the grill, we find ribs and potatoes and corn. We don't say much, beyond what's necessary, but I feel them both eyeing me with questions in every glance.

We eat on the back porch, watching the police cars roll by every ten minutes or so up and down the block. "Wow," says Bob, removing the fatty he rolled at some point during the preparations. "I think we should smoke this inside. No sense calling any kind of attention to ourselves, right?"

"Why all the cops," I ask.

"Honey, the downtown's in ruins," Debby reply. "Storefronts are, like, shattered. All the merchants are terrified of vandals. We heard it on the radio, the mayor's promised to crack down and protect all personal property."

"Come on." Bob gets to his feet and holds out his hand. "Let's go inside and light the sacred herb. It's time for Father Bob to hear your confession."

I laugh, surprised by how nervous I sound. "I've got nothing to confess."

Across the table, Debby snorts. "That's funny, honey. Because ever since we got to Stevie's house, you've been looking guilty as, like, all sin."

They let me have a few hits to gather my thoughts. Finally I pass the joint to Debby and let the last toke out in a long plume of white smoke. "You guys remember that day, right after we met, back when we worked for the government, and we were talking about the Dead, and I said something like there's music I can't listen to because it makes me feel physically sick?"

Bob and Debby glance at each other and shrug. "I guess," Debby answers for them both.

"Music did more than that for Stevie. He said listening to a Dead jam was like... having an orgasm for as long as the music lasted. But it wasn't just feelings and colors and sensations...at some point, Stevie learned how to see the math inside the music."

"The what?" asks Bob.

But Debby nods. "I remember once we were at the beach and he was listening to some jam, and I asked him what he could see, and he answered, 'Fractals, Debby, fractals."

"What the fuck's a fractal," asks Bob from a cloud of smoke.

"It's a geometric figure, each part of which has the same statistical character as the whole," answers Debby before I can speak.

"Huh?"

"Keep smoking, Bob, and maybe someday you'll understand." Debby tosses her mermaid curls over her shoulder.

"Fractals are patterns," I put in, before they come to blows. "They're infinite and always repeating...and if you uncover the basic structure, you can predict forward and backward from there. Once Stevie realized what he was he was seeing in the Dead's music, he realized...I guess... he realized... I don't know." I shake my head. "Look, maybe I can just show you."

I stand and pick up one of the flashlights. "Come on." I lead the way down the hall, through the house, to my bedroom. It used to be my great-grandfathers, and remained untouched until my grandmother died. She'd been keeping it as a shrine; I decided if I was going to try and hold on to the family home, I deserved the best room in the house.

So I spent a month stripping and steaming and painting the room a pale shade of coral pink, until Stevie offered to show me what he saw. "How," I remembered I asked, blankly. Even stoned, I had a hard time understanding what he was talking about.

"I can draw it," he said.

And so he had, one bright day in May, with the strains of my birthday present drifting through the room.

I push the door open wide, let Bob and Debby proceed me. "Go on," I say. "It's on the wall, to your left." I train the beam so that it falls as broadly as possible across the mural that goes from wall to wall, floor to ceiling. At first glance it's the painting of a naked woman on the bed across the room.

"Is that you, Mary Beth?" asks Bob, leaning closer.

"Of course it's Mary Beth," answers Debby. "But that's not paint, is it?" She beckons to me to bring the flashlight closer. "This is... this is different colored magic marker...and... Jesus... these are little equations...little... little math problems... look at this..."

"It's like Impressionism by number," quips Bob.

"You're so funny you must be high." Debby glances at me. "But who are all these other people? What's all this other stuff? Is this supposed to be the yellow brick road?"

"That's what the music made him see." I sink down on the bottom edge of the bed, training the beam of light on the wall. "Peter Max meet Albert Einstein."

"It's like if they had a kid," says Debby, plopping down next to me.

"Wow," says Bob, sitting on the other side.

For a long while, we sit, three in a row, the picture that compelling. He'd done parts of it in metallic marker and in the flashlight, the colors shimmer and shine with the same alien look as his attic.

A sultry breeze stirs the curtains, ruffles the Venetian blinds. The room grows warm, the heat rises between the spaces of our three bodies so close together. Perspiration begins to trickle down my sides, down my neck. Debby's bare skin next to mine feels damp, I smell Bob's sour sweat. But we can't look away.

Somehow, it feels more intimate than any sex I've ever had, with anyone, anywhere.

The night Stevie finished it, he stayed with me, the first night we'd shared in a long time. It was hot that night, too; too hot to sleep, too hot to touch. So we lay side by side, like a long-married couple, and finally, towards dawn, he beckoned me to join him on the edge of the bed.

At first I didn't understand what he wanted. He put his finger against my lips, hushing me, as the gray light blushed into dawn. "Just look," he whispered. "And tell me what if you hear it."

"Hear it?" I remember I looked, from him to the wall and back.

"Humor me," he said.

So I did, watching the light brighten, the picture shift, and subtly change. And just as the first golden spears of light made the shafts of dust mote dance in the space between us and the wall, I heard it.

Softly at first, and then stronger, I heard the unmistakable strains of the Dead's *Uncle John's Band* winding its way into my mental ear. I remember how I turned to Stevie with what must've been wonder in my eyes.

He smiled back at me like a virgin discovering sex. "You hear it, don't you?" he whispered. "You hear it... you really do."

"Oh my God," whispers Debby beside me. "The longer I stare at this... I swear I can hear something... I hear..."

"Come hear Uncle Johns' Band," sings Bob softly. "By the river side." He stops singing, looks at me. "Why that song?"

"That's what he was listening to, while he was doing it."

"You really posed naked for him?"

"No," I shake my head. "That's how he sees people. Everyone. He only sees clothes as... shadows... shadows that get in the way of energetic vibrations."

"How the hell do you sleep?" asks Debby.

"It stops if the room gets dark." I snap the flashlight off, and the music stops immediately. I snap it on again, but project the beam at the ceiling. "Fortunately I don't actually spend a lot of time in my bedroom. And when I am in here, I don't spend a lot of time staring at the wall."

"Oh, my God," says Debby, staring from the scrap of paper she pulls from her pocket, and the equations on the walls. "You know those numbers on the equipment up in Stevie's attic? Maybe they're time stamps... I'm not saying they're not. But without the divisions, without the zeros... if you look at them as just as a sequence of numbers...they're something else."

I point the flashlight down, so the scrap of paper is illuminated. "Okay," I say dubiously.

"What do you want us to see, Deb?" asks Bob, a tad impatiently.

"These numbers... 112358, 132134, 55, 89, 144... these are Fibonacci numbers..." She nods at the wall. "Stevie's ceiling was covered with them...and that picture is made of them."

"Wow," says Bob, just as there was a hard knock on the front door downstairs. He rises, peers out the window to his left, which is the side that overlooks the street below. "Fuck, it's the police."

IV

They know. There's no way they don't. We stink of weed. But the cops have way bigger fish to fry, so to speak, and they're not interested in keeping the population off drugs. In fact, sedated or stoned is probably how they'd like us all to be.

"The bridges are closed," the taller officer announces as soon as I open the door. "We're letting everyone still left on the island know that one of the big waves that rolled through during the storm damaged the supports –"

"Of every bridge?" interrupts Debby. "All three?"

"All three, ma'am. That wave rolled right through the channel. We're amazed it didn't swamp every house on the both sides of the bay. But until the Army engineers have a chance to get a better look tomorrow, we can't allow traffic. So we're letting people know… there's a ferry starting at 9 AM tomorrow, but until then, we're cut off."

"Anyone here likely to need any medical assistance?" asks the second cop. He gazes at all of us in turn and I am quite certain he's assessing how likely we are to pass drug tests.

"We're good," I say, and Debby and Bob murmur agreement. "We're all good."

The cop hesitates. I know him slightly – he's one of the Romero brothers. "Yeah," he says finally. "I can see you are." He taps his buddy on the shoulder, and they walk back down the sand-strewn walk, footsteps crunching in the dark.

"Thank God," breathes Debby. "Dodged that bullet."

"I don't know there's any thanking God about it," I snap. "They had to have smelled us. They might be back, when the town's cleaned up."

"They've got a lot more to worry about than a few stoned Deadheads, Mary Beth." Bob pats my shoulder.

"Come on," Debby tugs on my arm. "You haven't even begun to tell the story, yet. Back upstairs, missy."

On the way back to the kitchen, I stop in the living room and retrieve a CD. I place it in the center of the table. "That's what Stevie gave me for my birthday this year. It's a version of the Englishtown concert. And since he knew I didn't enjoy it … he made me a version he said I would enjoy."

"What?" Bob picks up the CD and examines it in the light of the candles Debby's lighting around the kitchen. "He managed to get rid of Donna somehow?"

"More than that, Bob. He ... he took all the recordings of the concert ever made and somehow pulled apart every instrument and then put them all back together ...at least, everyone I wanted to hear." I pick up the CD. "But when you listen to it... it's not like any recording you've ever heard. He...distilled the sound in some way... I don't know how to explain it. He...purified it... that's the only way I can describe it."

"I got to hear this," say Bob.

"Fuck yeah," agrees Debby. "You have a CD player that runs on batteries?"

Before I can shake my head, there's another knock on the door, this time on the back door, the one that leads up the steps from the alley.

"Shit," says Debby. "That cop's back."

Bob puts the ashtray on a chair. "What the ..."

I open the door. It's the Romero brother, and his partner. "Hi, officers. How can I help you?"

They glance at each other, clear their throats. "You all mind letting us in? We have some questions about the whereabouts of Steven Garracino."

"Let's talk outside," says Debby, pushing through the screen door. "It's really hot in there."

"I'm calling Bernie," says Bob, melting into the dark.

It turns out that Stevie's neighbor, Agnes Annarelli, is the dispatcher on duty. And now that the old town's been buttoned down tighter than a nun's underwear, she's remembered that her poor dear neighbor's son has gone AWOL, probably because of the pot-smoking degenerates he's gotten involved with.

They're looking at both me and Debby like specimens under a glass. "We don't know where Stevie is," I say. "We've been trying to figure that out ourselves."

"Why didn't you notify the police?"

"We're not sure how long he's been gone," I reply, refusing to be intimidated.

"And in case you guys haven't noticed," says Debby, "there's been a national type disaster, in the last forty-eight hours."

"One of our friends thinks Stevie may have been upset," I say. "The rest of us…well, we're not sure."

"So you're saying you think he could've hurt himself?"

"I have a hard time believing that," I say. "He takes care of his mom… he wouldn't do that to her."

"Thanks, I appreciate that," says a voice from behind the policemen.

"Oh, my God," says Debby, pushing past the cops. "Stevie Garracino, do you know how worried we've all been?"

"Where'd you get to, man?" asks Bob, coming through the screen door, with a look of purest relief.

I'm hanging back, too stunned, too shocked to say anything. Debby's hugging him, the cops are shrugging, turning to leave, letting Stevie past on their way down the steps. Their work here, at least tonight, is done. Thank God.

Stevie's clothes are drenched, there's sand and bits of what look sea-weed and seashells in his hair. He's unshaven, and he looks different, somehow, as he staggers a little as he puts down his old black duffel bag. I don't think I've ever been so relieved to see anyone in my life. "Stevie?" I say at last, as Debby pulls away. "You…you okay?"

He reaches for me, wraps his arms around me, and pulls me close. He smells like the beach, his clothes feel stiff, like they've been soaked in salt water and dried. "Oh, Mary Beth," he whispers against my hair. "You won't believe what a long strange trip it's been."

V

We get him inside, give him some food, pass him a beer, then a joint. Finally he comes up for air. "My mom okay?"

"She's great," says Bob. "Worried as shit about you, man. Bernadette's got her. You should call her, let her know. Don't you think?"

"I already did," says Debby. "Just to say you were safe. I told them you were starving... your mom says to let you eat."

"Really?" says Stevie. "I thought she'd be pissed at shit."

"Well, she is," says Debby. "She wouldn't actually get on the phone. Bernadette said that."

"That's more like it." He mops up the last of the barbeque sauce on his plate.

"So how long are you going to hold out on us, buddy?" asks Bob. "Where the fuck have you been? Your mom might be the reincarnation of Attila the Hun but I got to tell you...that just wasn't cool, leaving her like that."

Stevie meets Bob's eyes. "You really think I left her alone on purpose?"

"Nah, man," Bob shakes his head. "You know I don't. But you got us good and scared. So where were you, and what happened?"

Stevie takes one more hit of the joint, a long one, and lets it out slowly. "This would be way easier if I could show you."

"Show us what?" I ask.

To our complete astonishment, he pulls a cassette tape out of his pocket. "This." He looks around. "I need my duffel bag."

"There," I say, pointing to a corner of the kitchen.

"Great."

As Stevie retrieves it, Bob hands each of us a joint. "I have a feeling we're each going to need our own for this."

"You heard the wall," I say. "This can't be too much more far out." I look over to the counter, where Stevie is setting up his boom box. "Ready?"

Stevie nods. He slips the tape into its deck then turns to us. "So... bear with me, guys? Mary Beth has heard some of this. Okay. You remember how Huxley wrote about how mescaline opened up doors in his mind....the doors of perception, he called them...doors through which he could glimpse other dimensions. Right?"

We nod. We know this.

"Most modern music follows very simple patterns and structures. That's why so much of it sounds alike. But when Jerry improvised, he didn't stick to those simple patterns and structures... he spun off them in such a way that something in the structure of the sound in the music he creates... totally spontaneously and in the moment... those very structures ARE the doors of perception. Or at least, pieces of them, parts of them." He pauses, eyes shining, face alight. "Most people need drugs of some kind to perceive the doors are there... Huxley needed mescaline; Bob, I believe you prefer 'ludes." He looks at me and winks. "I know what Mary Beth likes."

"So, wait, back up," says Debby. "You're saying that basically these doors that Huxley wrote about are real? Or can be real if you listen to Jerry's jams in the right frame of mind?"

Stevie pauses, cocks his head. "They're real...and yes, in the right state of mind...you perceive the doors, and possibly something beyond them."

"All right," says Bob. "Go on."

"The reason most people need drugs to help is because each improvisation only contains a tiny amount of information, kind of like a byte of information on a computer chip, or a single brick in a whole wall. So I started by taking all the Dead shows, and laying them out linearly. I tracked both the simple patterns that form the underlying basis of the song, and then the more complex ones Jerry creates in his improvisations."

"And what were you looking for again?" I ask.

"Fibonacci patterns, overlapping Fibonacci patterns, places where his leads intersected with all the instruments in very precise and measurable sound waves that perfectly correlated to Fibonacci sequences –"

"Why?" asks Debby. "Why Fibonacci patterns? I remember you told me when you heard music you saw fractals."

"Fractals are made of Fibonacci sequences," Stevie answers. "Fractals are the building blocks of reality. And the highest incidences of these sequences always come right before, during and after the space jams."

"When, like, you really can feel reality expanding all around you," murmurs Debby, "and you don't exactly know why."

"Well, if you remembered what drugs you took, you remember why," says Bob.

"It's not just about drugs, Bob," I say. "It's why the drugs work so well."

"Exactly," says Stevie. "You get a gold star." Our eyes meet and he smiles at me, differently, somehow. "So...I figured that, if these doors that Jerry's music is able to somehow access really are integral to the structure of reality - if they really do exist, then they can't exist without all their parts." He pauses, takes a hit of his joint. "So I thought that maybe, if I could create a vacuum in the music, in those parts where the Fibonacci sequences exist, then Jerry – or the part of Jerry that makes the music - would come to fill it, because the structure of reality depends upon it."

We all smoke in silence, digesting.

"I tried just stripping Jerry out of those places, totally cutting out his leads. Then I'd record them, and let them play over and over, for days, even weeks. And I recorded the recordings, hoping to pick up something... anything... that could fill the space in the music I made." He shakes his head. "But it didn't work. No matter what I came up with to try, it didn't work."

He pauses, less for dramatic effect and more for another toke. "I realized that all the subtle sounds of the environment, the house, the cars outside, my mother's TV, even my own equipment was creating enough of a vibration to fill the space. I realized my Fibonacci sequences need some boosting... something bigger than any drug I could take or piece of equipment I could buy. That was my breakthrough."

"What?" we all ask, almost together.

"The ocean. The waves. I thought maybe... if I went out as far as I could get, away from the shore, but still near the waves, I figured I'd inevitably catch a few sequences that matched. If you create the right conditions, patterns will start to link up, and synchronize. I figured if

I could catch the ocean waves pounding out a sequence...well... maybe the door would open wide enough for something to come through loudly enough for my equipment to pick it up. Because that was the other problem I wasn't sure I was having....that possibly my equipment just wasn't that sensitive.

"So that's what I did. I invested in the best double-track boom box I could find." He pats the box on the counter.

"That piece of shit?" Bob points.

"It looked a lot better before the storm."

"Wait," Debby says. "So you were... you really were out in the storm?"

"Oh, Deb," Stevie says, looking contrite as an altar boy caught with his hand in his pants. "I think I caused the storm... or, if not the storm, I think what I did made it worse." We begin to protest, but he continues, "No, seriously, listen to me. So I took this boom box, and two tapes... one, a continuous loop of the *Eyes of the World* jam from the Englishtown concert, and a blank one....out to the end of the 18th Street pier."

"The fishing pier? The one with the little bunker at the very end of it?"

"The one they rebuilt after Hurricane Sandy. And they did a good job, because let me tell you, if they hadn't, I wouldn't be alive." He pats the box again. "And I wouldn't have this."

"So go on," says Bob.

"I knew rain was predicted, I knew the waves would be a little churned up. I waited until dark, then took my box and my tapes and set myself up at the edge of the pier. It wasn't too bad, for quite a while, and then the waves really started to pick up. I knew the rhythm I was hoping to hear...and a few times it started to build. So I thought I might be on to something."

"So you stayed," I say. "While it got worse?"

"By the time I figured I better get off the pier, I really couldn't. I got inside the bunker, and hunkered down, best I could, under a pile of tarps. The windows blew out... but the pilings and the roof and the walls held. Eventually the storm died down, and I fell asleep. When I woke up, I had another problem... from the pier I could see how badly everything had flooded. The water was up to the tops of the cars, so I had to wait until it went down.

"And by that time...the place was crawling with National Guard, who insisted on taking me to their hospital tent. So by the time they let me go, and I walked all the way home... they had closed off my block, and when they wouldn't let me go home...I came here."

"You're lucky to be alive." For the first time, I feel something of the exasperation Mrs. G must feel for her son.

"You know, Mary Beth, you're right. What I did was crazy, it was insane. But if I hadn't done it, I wouldn't have... this." He presses the play button, and adjusts the volume. The sounds of waves crashing against the pier fills the room, along with an eerie wail. Along with the weather though, is a song even I recognize; the introduction is unmistakable to any Deadhead.

"'Wake up to find out you are the eyes of the world,'" Bob sings.

"Shut up," the rest of us say. It's weird to realize your own mind is filling in the missing parts.

"Here it comes," whispers Stevie.

In unison, we lean forward, clustering close. The candles throw up weird shadows on the walls, the night is completely still. I realize, suddenly, just how quiet it is, with no passing traffic, no ambient noise off the street.

And out of the void, out of the emptiness, out of the space where no music was a second ago and where no music should be, the faintest echo of a riff dances through the air.

"Oh, my God," whispers Bob. "It's different. It's a lead... but it's different."

"It's, like, completely different," breathes Debby, bug-eyed.

I don't say anything, because I can't. I can hear what Stevie's done and I can't talk around the lump in my throat, the chills down my back.

We gaze at each other around the table, holding our breaths, listening to a lead that only Jerry Garcia could play but that we all know full well Jerry Garcia didn't play...not in Englishtown, New Jersey, in May of 1977, anyway.

The notes don't last very long. There's a crackle, then a hiss. "Oh, shit," says Stevie. He snaps the recorder off.

The impossible music hangs silently in the air.

"Wow," says Bob, eventually. "I guess you did it."

Stevie nods, looking a lot less upset than I expect. "Yeah. I guess I did. I knew I should've waited...hopefully I can get this cleaned up."

We glance at each other. We're all exhausted but I know we're all thinking about Stevie's ruined attic. Bob, that coward, gets up. "You know... this is really cool and all...I want hear more... but tomorrow. Okay with you, Mary Beth?"

"Sure," I say. Leave me to the bearer of bad news.

"Me, too, Mary Beth." Debby gets to her feet. "I have to go stare at the ceiling before all this makes any sense."

"Go right ahead," I say. I can't imagine how I'm going to break the news to Stevie that everything – or as close to everything as we could tell – is irreparably damaged.

But when we're alone, he doesn't ask about the attic. Instead he asks about me. "I'm good," I reply. There's something different about him, something I can't quite put my finger on. "A little worried about the plants, but less so now that I'm sure your mother's not going to send the police here looking for you."

"We'll figure out the plants," he says. He coves my hand with his.

I can't hold out any longer. "Stevie, when we went over to your place, we went up to the attic. And I really hate to tell you... the door must've blown open at some point. Everything was ... well... wet. The post-its were all blown around. I just want to prepare you. You may not have the equipment any more to... to fix that."

And to my surprise, he shrugs. "It's okay. The project's over. I did what I set out to do. It's time I got off my fucking ass and do something useful."

"Really?" This really is a different Stevie.

"Yeah. I was thinking of going back to school, maybe get a degree in math, or quantum physics. Figure out how to help people with this stuff I've figured out. After all, what else is all it for?"

I'm happy for the first time in at least a couple days, maybe in a lot longer. The last of the candles is starting to sputter, the ocean air is turning cool. "I'm glad you're okay," I say. His hand is still on mine, and I twine my fingers with his. "You must be exhausted. What do you say we go listen to my wall?"

The End

Walking with Elvis

———

Celebrity Supernatural #4

After "The Cremation of Sam McGee"
— With apologies to Robert L. Service

"There are strange things done in the midnight sun by the men who moil for gold;
   The arctic trails have their secret tales that would make your blood run cold.
The Northern Lights have seen strange sights but the strangest they ever did see
Was that night in Maine, from the wreck of the train, we hunted down Elvis Presley."

I

Grandpa arrived clutching the telegram, just as Grandma was putting the remains of last night's pot roast on the table. It was two days before Christmas, and the tail end of the second blizzard in five days had finally stopped moaning around the eaves. He entered on a gust that blew a swirl of snow all the way to the living room before it evaporated in the heat of the wood-burning stove.

"I'll need to be up early," he said, as he kicked off his boots, and hung up his parka. He brushed the snow off the beard that made him look a little like Abraham Lincoln, and dropped a kiss on my grandmother's rosy cheek. "You're so young and beautiful," he crooned. "You're everything to me." From inside his sweater vest, he whipped out a pale pink rose tied with a silver ribbon. "Happy anniversary a day early, Mrs. B," he said with a wink at me.

Grandma giggled like the sixteen year old she'd been when they met. For as long as I could remember, Grandma resembled Mrs. Butterworth to the degree that when I was five, I thought she *was* Mrs. Butterworth and told my entire kindergarten class that the syrup bottle lady was my grandma. I might have been seventeen but I could count on that story being rolled out whenever I was home from boarding school, like an old ornament that refused to break. "Now that's young and beautiful." She returned a quick kiss on his lips, then dodged his embrace. "That pelt on your face is all wet...I wish you'd get rid of that thing."

"Keep's my face warm." Grandpa winked at me, then my sixteen year old cousin Travis, who was visiting from Boston for the holiday. "Pass that stew, young man." He ladled out a dripping bowlful then glanced at Grandma, who'd taken her place at the other end of the table. "Do me a favor after supper, Nellie, and call down to Elise at the hotel? She's about to get slammed."

Grandma put the basket of buttermilk biscuits in front of Travis, then slapped his hand as he reached into it. "Don't tell me the annual meeting's still on? Even after all this snow? Are the tracks even clear north of Bangor?"

"The annual bacchanalia," my grandfather said with a short laugh that didn't sound amused. While snow at Christmas wasn't unusual in our carved out little corner of Maine, over fifty inches had fallen in two back to back storms in the last five days. Grandpa was the station master and it was his job – among others – to make sure the train tracks were clear at all times. "The show must go on." He glanced at me, then at Travis. "Forget I said that, boys." He gestured to the basket. "Pass the biscuits. And the butter?"

"May we say grace, please?" asked Grandma, holding out her hands.

We bowed our heads. By the time we said Amen, my mouth was watering. Anything that wasn't cooked in the school cafeteria tasted heavenly to me. Travis was just hungry…we'd spent most of the day keeping the driveway shoveled out.

For a few minutes, we were all too hungry to talk. My grandmother watched us with a satisfied expression. She waited until my grandfather reached for his third biscuit. Then she nodded at the envelope sticking out of the pocket of his vest, the one with Western Union emblazoned on the corner. "You got a telegram, John?"

"From the Overseer. Confirming the arrival of the shareholders, as scheduled…and that the new President and Vice-President, as well as some members of Congress will be among this year's guests."

Even Travis stopped eating when he heard that. "You mean the new President as in… the new President of the United States? As in… Ronald Reagan?"

My grandfather took a long look at Travis. Grandpa cleared his throat and carefully split his biscuit into two pieces. "We like to call him the Gipper around here."

Travis looked back at him blankly.

"You know," said my grandmother, "from the Knute Rockne movie? Ronald Reagan played the Gipper?"

Travis looked from Grandma, to Grandpa then back to me. "My dad says just because someone's good at pretending to be something doesn't mean they really are."

The tick of the cuckoo was the only answer. My grandmother stared at her plate. My grandfather's expression belonged on Mount Rushmore. Travis looked at me, with an expression that reminded me of the dorm's dog when he wanted to go out.

He was the closest thing I was ever likely to have to a brother, and I felt not only compelled to help, but overall responsible for his having a good time. It was a real treat – or supposed to be – for my grandparents to have him visit, and no small amount of planning and preparation had gone into it. So I put down my fork, cleared my throat, and looked at my grandmother. "Me and Travis found a bunch of 45's up in the attic, Grandma. If you don't mind, I thought after dinner me and him could sort them out, see if any are still playable. And then I thought we could bring down a few and you and Grandpa can show us how to cut a rug."

My mother was planning to throw my grandparents a fortieth wedding anniversary surprise party at the train station. A 1950's style sock-hop was the theme. One of the benefits of working for the Company was that all the entertainers who stayed at the Compound performed for us on their way there. My grandmother had fallen in love with Elvis back in 1959, when he'd singled her out to sing "Love Me Tender" to from the back of the train. She even thought Grandpa looked like Elvis when he didn't have his beard. And maybe he did, if Elvis had managed to stay thin, in shape, and alive.

My job was to find as many old records as I could so they could be played on the old juke box my mom was having brought over from the bar.

"Well, of course," Grandma said. "Nothing I like more than a twirl or two to Elvis." She smiled at Grandpa, then to my relief, at Travis. "You know, I do think your grandpa looks a bit like Elvis...when he doesn't have that beard, that is. Makes me fall in love with him again every spring, when he shaves it off, it does. In fact, Travis... now I think of it... you look a little bit like Elvis, too. You've got the chin... the mouth... and those eyes...Don't you think, John? What do you say, Johnny?"

Travis smiled tentatively, I agreed enthusiastically, and Grandpa grunted.

"John," said Grandma. "I was thinking maybe Johnny should go along with you tomorrow...see a bit more of what's what..."

"What's what is going to be cold, and snowy and wet," replied my grandfather. "There won't be anything to see. I'll be out of here before dawn, and back before noon, with any luck at all...I want to rest up for the Christmas Eve festivities. The Gipper's going to speak to the town for a few minutes after the Overseer's address. Nick wants everyone there at least thirty minutes before the train's due in."

"I think he'd better tell everyone an hour," Grandma said. "You know how long it can some of the younger families to get themselves together."

"Who's Nick?" Travis asked me.

"Town Manager," I answered, through a bite.

"And who is this overseer, and why do you all seem so afraid of him?" Travis continued. My mouth was too full to interrupt and I nearly choked on what he said next. "The only overseers I've ever heard about were on slave plantations and in concentration camps. Why do you people have an overseer?"

"Come on, Travis," I said, swallowing as fast as I could. "Let's go sort the records, then we can go tell my mom about the Gipper." I moved fast out of the dining room, avoiding my grandfather's gaze, kissing my grandmother on the cheek.

Travis followed my lead, bolting up the steps after me to my third floor bedroom. "What the hell, man... slow up."

I picked up a carton we carried from the attic that afternoon and dumped it on the end of the twin bed he was sleeping in.

"I don't get it," Travis said, as I started sorting through the black discs, looking for any obviously warped or scratched. "All I did was ask a question. What's so wrong with asking questions?"

I nodded at the second carton. "You go through those... we'll see if we can get them down to one box... and then we'll take them down to Mom. It's time to get you out the house, I can tell."

"Johnny...what the fuck, man?" Travis paused. He was as tall as I was, only not as broad. "I'm not fucking six. I don't need to be taken out of the house."

"Could you just sort?"

Travis took a deep breath. "You didn't answer me. What's wrong with asking questions? Don't you ever ask any questions?"

It was my turn to pause, take a deep breath and consider what to say. "No," I answered, as evenly and reasonably as I could. "I don't."

We finished the records in silence. Most seemed perfectly fine to me, so I set aside a few to show Grandma. We carried the cartons downstairs, and left them in the dark foyer, so Grandma wouldn't see us take them from the house. She was in the kitchen, finishing up the dishes.

"I'm sorry we didn't stay to help," I said, with a contrite kiss. "I'm so used to ditching my tray and heading to the dorm for the good spot in front of the TV I forgot you might want some help."

"It's all right, honey," she replied. "You go on, both of you... I called your mom... she's expecting you. And here, Travis, honey, take this dish, will you?"

"I'm sorry if I upset you and Grandpa," he said.

"We won't talk any more about it," she said, with a swift caress of his cheek. "You didn't mean anything by it. We both knew that." She turned back to the sink. "Don't fill up on pretzels and beer, now. There'll be cookies and cocoa waiting here when you get back."

"Thanks, Grandma, bye Grandma."

We bundled up once more, picked up our boxes, and stepped out into a night that glittered from the sky to the snow. The moon, just past the full, hung low over the black tips of the trees like a bloated belly. The snow crunched beneath our boots, our breath hung in the air. The glow of the streetlights illuminated the few stray flakes still falling. A few streets over, I heard the scrape and whir of the Company snow plows.

There're some who believe that Stanton's Fall was the inspiration for Thornton Wilder's Grover's Corners, and that may very well be. A lot of famous people have rolled through Stanton's Fall, one way or another. And the town does resemble the description of Grover's Corners, sort of, with the cemetery overlooking the town, the green with the church at one end and a white gazebo at the other, a Main Street networked to a neat grid of tidy streets.

As we turned the corner, heading toward the center of town, Travis started. "This sure is an amazing place," he said. "Everything's so neat and clean and perfect... it almost doesn't look real."

"The snow makes it look like Fairyland," I agreed, cautiously.

"And when there's no snow, it looks like Disneyland. You ever been to Disney, Johnny?" Travis doesn't wait for me to answer. "Have you ever realized that Main Street looks exactly like the one in Disney?"

"I guess I don't have to go, then," I said. Tiny flakes of snow stung my cheeks. "We don't have a lot of money for vacations, Travis. The Company takes us all to the beach for three weeks every year, and the kids all get to go to camp. And married people, old people, they get to go to the Company island in the Bahamas, for honeymoons and stuff. But no one has money for vacations to places like Disney, Travis. It must be nice that you do."

If Travis understood I insulted him, he didn't react. Instead he pushed on. "But that's the point, Johnny. No one seems to have money for anything. They even told me how much money I could bring...and then, anything I hadn't spent by the time I got to Bangor, they made me give it all to the guy who met me there. He wouldn't even let me get in the car with it."

"There's nothing here to buy, Travis. We're not a tourist town... We're a Company town. You didn't come for the souvenirs, you came to see your family. What's weird about that?"

For a second Travis halted under a street light, his whole body illuminated by the shaft of falling snow. "What's weird about it? Johnny... what's normal about it?"

"I don't get to keep money at school, Travis." I turned around, shifting the carton to my opposite shoulder.

"And speaking of school, don't you ever wonder... why the son of a bar maid and a truck driver gets to go to one of the most expensive schools in the entire USA? Maybe in the entire world? Don't you ever wonder why?"

For a split second I wanted to throw my carton on the ground and go for his throat. And then I remembered what my grandmother said, just before Travis arrived. "He's not going to understand a lot about our ways," she said. "He might say things about your mother, about us, that hurt your feelings. But try to remember he wasn't raised in our ways. Try to remember he's just a stranger in a very strange land, and we have to ...make allowances."

And I had, after all, just insulted him. So I swallowed my rage and cleared my throat. "What's got into you, Travis? Can't you just relax and enjoy our time together? Can't you see how happy Grandma is to have you here? It's all she's been talking about for weeks. It wasn't exactly easy to get you approved to come, let me tell you. You ought to try and be a little more grateful." I turned on my heel and started off.

Travis hurried after me. "I am... I am grateful, of course I am. It's just ...I've never seen anything like this, outside of Disney. Don't you have any idea how fucking perfect it all is?"

We came to another corner, and this time we were forced to stop long enough to let a couple snow plows roll by. They were painted in the Company's colors of red and white, and they added to the Christmas gloss the town's wearing. We were right at the edge of the town center, and the street lights were all festooned with evergreens and plaid ribbons in the Company colors. I gazed down the street, toward the church at the end of the green, and I understood something of what Travis is talking about.

Against the background of the freshly fallen snow, Stanton's Fall was picture perfect, from the frosted pines, to the Christmas lights twinkling on porches and in windows. Except for the plows, the town was silent, every house shuttered tight against the storm.

And I've been through Bangor and Boston and New York on my way back and forth to school. Stanton's Fall is about as different from any of those places as it's possible to be. "You know, Travis, just because this place isn't like what you're used to...lots of places aren't as gritty as Boston."

"This's got nothing to do with grit." We started across the street. Travis shifted his own carton from shoulder to shoulder and continued. "This place is like Xanadu, and you're all too stoned to see it."

The only reason I didn't hit him is because Grandma won't like it if Travis comes home with a black eye. "Someone's been reading their tenth grade poetry."

"You make fun of me all you want." We trudged almost another block in silence, and then he continued, "Speaking of stoned... I don't suppose there's any chance..."

"Are you kidding?" I stopped in my tracks. "Are you fucking out of your mind? Didn't you have to take a drug test to visit?"

Travis didn't answer.

I actually felt sorry for him. "C'mon. Legal drinking age around here is sixteen."

He whipped his head up and around, then shook it. "Cut it out. I know you're fucking with me."

"No, I'm not. My mom will give us at least a half pint each... maybe even a pint. Someone has to keep the kids happy around here when they're home."

"What do you mean... when they're home?"

I pointed down the street, toward the town green, where the nativity display for the town crèche has disappeared under a mountain of snow taller than we are. "Everyone around here goes away somewhere for high school, Trav. We have to. School only goes to eighth grade. Town's too small for a high school." I paused to swallow another surge of anger. "That's how the son of a bar maid and a truck driver gets to go to prep school." You fucking ass. I left that out, but it hit me, then, that Travis's views weren't just his...this was what my uncle thought of his sister, of me.

I strode off, suddenly furious.

"Hey...hey...Johnny...I'm sorry." It finally occurred to Travis he'd stuck his foot in his mouth. It occurred to me that no wonder my uncle couldn't work for the Company if his son was at all like him.

I didn't turn around, just kept walking, until I heard him slide and fall behind me. Then I turned around. "Serves you right, asshole."

"I'm sorry." He offered his hand from the ground. "Shake?"

"Sure." Grudgingly I shook. Grudgingly I helped him up. It wasn't his fault he was an ass. I'd heard my grandfather use that word quite a few times to describe my uncle in the days before Travis's arrival. We walked the rest of the way to the hotel in silence.

Guests of the Company stayed at the Compound but sometimes they have drivers, secretaries, people like that who need a place to stay. And there are truckers who come through, once or twice a month, bringing supplies and other things. That's how my mother met my father. And yes, she's a barmaid, or rather, bartender, but she went to prep school, too: Miss Porter's, to be exact.

My mother was wiping down the bar when we come in. "Hey, you." She looked up, surprised. "I didn't think you'd be out in this."

"We needed to get out of the house." I nodded, just once, in Travis's direction. "And Grandpa wanted me to let you know he got a telegram… the shareholders are coming in spite of the snow."

"Oh, yeah," she replied. "Nick Cabot stopped by…we're getting the place all put together … you never know who's going to be looking at what, you know? Travis, honey, how are you doing? You getting sick of watching the snow fall and the dust settle yet?"

"Hi, Aunt Elise." Travis's Boston accent was especially thick. "We brought you records."

"Perfect," she said. "Just stick them over there."

"Most of this whole box is nothing but Elvis, Mom," I said, placing my box beside Travis's.

"That's all right," my mother said. "You know how Grandma loves Elvis. Elvis's has always been a big hit here in Stanton's Fall…the shareholders were just crazy about Elvis."

II

Next day was Christmas Eve. By the time Travis and I woke up, Grandpa was long gone. After breakfast, I went down to the hotel to help my mother, while Grandma amused Travis with photo albums.

Maybe it was bright sun, maybe it was what Travis said last night, but the whole town did have a particularly shiny glaze to it. Maybe it was just the coating of ice and snow.

It bothered me that my uncle and my cousin and presumably my aunt looked down on my mother, on me, on my grandparents. What was wrong with working for the Company, I wondered as I retraced our footsteps from last night. In the aftermath of the blizzard, in anticipation of Christmas Eve, it seemed like the whole town was outside, shoveling, gossiping, fine-turning decorations, sledding.

It took me twice as long to get to the hotel as last night because I had to stop and talk to so many people. What was wrong with Travis, I wondered. The whole town was so neat and clean and beautiful. There was no crime, no poverty, nothing that hinted at anything of the dark side of the world. We were given good educations, houses in which to live and raise our families… and work.

No one ever worried about finding a job in Stanton's Fall, unlike my aunt and uncle, who'd been out of work on and off in the last ten years. I don't think that ever happens here, I told him.

"Why don't Uncle Cole and Aunt Lacey ever come here?" I asked my mother as I helped her hoist and carry and shift.

"They're not welcome," my mother replied, pointing a flashlight at the back of the barn beside the hotel.

"Well, why not?"

"In case you haven't realized it, Johnny, your uncle disappointed a lot of people and devastated your grandparents."

"But… but…." I fumbled for the words. I'm really not good at asking questions; it's something perceived as a lack by my teachers, although it doesn't bother anyone here. "It's not like… it's not like they're bad people… he's a history teacher, she teaches music. Travis is … a loudmouth but he's basically okay. Why aren't they welcome?"

My mother straightened and touched my cheek. "Because they're not Company people, Johnny. There're two kinds of people in this world: Company people, and everybody else. And trust me when I tell you, it's us against them. The rest of the world… they might look down on us, but believe me, most of them would give their eyeteeth to live the way we do. Your uncle walked away from everything and he didn't just walk away; he did it in the most hurtful way possible. So trust me when I tell you, he's not welcome here. And the only reason Travis is here at all is because of the very high regard the Company has for your grandparents. Now bring those boxes over to the kitchen, and then put that ladder away."

With that she walked away, leaving me in the dark.

We worked until one, walked home together and ate a late lunch-early supper of clam chowder and corn fritters, glistening with fat fresh from the fryer. Then my mother walked back to the hotel to ready the final preparations.

With a couple hours to kill, Grandma brought out a plate of the cookies she and Travis had baked that morning, and suggested we find something to watch on TV. "Find something to amuse yourselves, and try to stay out of trouble... I'm going up to take my nap."

We settled on the living room floor. Before Grandma went upstairs, she bent over and kissed both of us on the top of our heads. "My handsome boys," she smiled down. "Handsome as your grandfather."

Travis was the guest so I handed hm the remote. He started clicking through the channels, but almost predictably started to complain. "What kind of channels are these? What happened to CBS and all? What the hell is NNN?"

"NNN is News Now Network. We're too far away from anywhere to pick up regular channels, so the Company gives us channels to watch... without any stupid commercials. Look." I take the remote, and show him the menu. "See? There's a kids' channel... there's a Christmas channel... here's the movie channel..."

"It's playing an Elvis movie." Travis stood up. "Come on, Johnny, get your head out of your ass, will you? This town is like the land that time forgot... it's like you're all stuck in 1959."

"Where are you going?" I asked, as he crossed the room.

"I might as well work on my homework...I have a book to read for school."

"Yeah? What?"

"Lord of the Flies." He disappeared up the steps two at a time, leaving me watching Elvis dance his way through Las Vegas.

I got up, went to the window, and watched the blowing snow. I thought I would like having Travis around, looked forward to his visit, but part of me wished he'd go away. He made me uncomfortable with all his questions, put Grandma on edge and made Grandpa... almost angry. I looked up and down the street. The neighborhood kids had joined forces and were having a snow ball fight. I thought about going outside and joining in, but I figured I better stay inside and keep an eye on Travis, since that was basically what Grandma had told me to do.

As the head boy on my floor the previous year, and then my entire dorm that year, I'd become used to looking out for younger, dumber kids – like it was my job. So even if Travis hadn't been my cousin, hadn't felt like the annoying younger brother for which I was rapidly becoming grateful I'd never had, I think that's why I still feel so guilty, so responsible for everything that happened to him.

III

My grandfather left at three, so he wasn't home at 4 when the rest of us headed to the train station for the annual festivities and, as it turned out the surprise anniversary party, which was really only a surprise for Grandma, Grandpa having been in on it all along. Which was unfortunate because neither me nor Grandma thought to tell Travis he couldn't bring his camera.

The timing of the party was a complete surprise to all three of us – especially Grandma who blushed like a bride when she walked into the train station and saw Grandpa all gussied up and Nick Cabot the Town Manager waiting to marry them again. I suppose Travis forgot he had a camera, or maybe he thought the fortieth anniversary of two old codgers getting married didn't merit any pictures, or maybe he was just too busy being introduced to everyone in town.

As it happened, when he did whip it out, he was standing next to me, and I was too busy watching the train pull into town to notice. He was standing next to me because I wanted to show him my favorite vantage point, toward the very end of the platform, where you could still hear the Overseer's speech, but also see into the guest cars, where the guests had invariably started the party.

You couldn't ask for autographs or take pictures, but you could shake hands and talk to anyone who happened to stick his or her head out the window and be friendly. And because most of them had been partying since Boston, at least, most of them were feeling very friendly indeed. By the time I was Travis's age – and I don't mean to brag – I'd met every member of every rock band who ever hit the top of the charts, as well as a lot of movie and television stars. I figured if Travis got a look at all the people who came through Stanton's Fall, he wouldn't feel we were so out of touch.

The last strains of Love Me Tender were floating through the crisp evening air and the light on the engine had appeared in the darkness as we wandered out to the platform. Most people were clustering down at the opposite end, wanting to see and be seen by the Overseer. I pulled Travis all the way to the end, out of the glow of the last platform light. "With any luck at all, the first guest car will stop right about here."

I fill the silence between us with chatter about the movie stars I've met, the rock stars I've shaken hands with. "I even remember Jim Morrison," I said, because I knew how much Travis liked the Doors.

But instead of asking me anything I could've foreseen, Travis instead asked, "Have you ever been in the Compound?"

"Only to the gatehouse," I replied. It's a big deal to go to the Compound, even bigger than the high school graduation you go to celebrate. "Grandpa goes up there once in a while, to make sure deliveries get there and such, and a few times I've gone with him. But they don't let you past the gatehouse until you're 18."

"Don't you ever wonder why?"

"I know why," I retort, more vehemently than I mean to. "The question is, why do you care?" The pinprick of light in the distance that is the train is getting bigger and the crowd is getting larger, too, as more and more people come out of the Station House and crowd around the tracks. Everyone is turned away from us; we are standing on the edge of the dark lip of the platform.

"Because something happened in there, something happened that my father won't tell me. That's why my father left... whatever he saw made him go away. My father's not a bad person ...he wouldn't hurt anyone, not deliberately. But whatever happens in that Compound... whatever goes on in there... he won't tell me. He won't tell anyone."

There was no time to answer, because the light of the train was getting huge, the faint scream of a train whistle rising in the night. Everyone at the other end of the platform reacted, I shook my head at Travis, and then turned as the engine burst out of the woods, with a bellow and a burst of steam.

"Whoa," said Travis, his mouth hanging open. The train was black, sleek and new in 1878. I was glad something could shut him up.

As the train slowed to a crawl, the engineer and his mate waved. The cattle cars came immediately after the engine, cargo cars with long narrow windows near the ceilings and drains at the floors for the provisions. Then came the passenger cars filled with the secretaries and maids and other support staff that the shareholders and their guests required. More than half of them rose and got ready to get off as the train came to a screeching, shrieking halt.

"Stanton's Fall," shouted the conductor, who I'd known all my life. "Stanton's Fall." Luke Hammond's family have been conductors almost as long as mine have been Station Masters.

Travis tugged at my arm, then pointed to the cattle cars. "What's in those?"

At first I ignored him, because I was too busy peering into the windows of the shareholder cars, looking for faces I recognized from album covers and TV Guide. "Those are the people who work for the shareholders and the guests."

"No," he said. "The ones in front of those... the ones without the windows."

"Those are the cattle cars... I don't know... they have luggage and stuff. Why?"

"Because why are they unloading barrels marked Medical Waste?" And at that, Travis did the unbelievable. He pointed to the front of the train, where a group of shadowy workers materialized out of the darkness. In the stark light of a lone street lamp, they began unloading barrels off the backs of the cattle cars. Before I could stop him, Travis whipped out of his camera and snapped a photograph.

In the darkness, the flash went off like a star.

"Stop that," I said. I grabbed for the camera, but Travis was too quick for me.

He wasn't quick enough for the men who tackled us both.

I came to in my grandfather's office inside the Station House. Through the thick glass, I could hear cheering, and I had to assume the Overseer was giving his speech. Travis was sitting in the leather wing chair beside mine, shaking his head, rubbing his jaw. My grandfather was sitting across from us, on the other side of his desk, watching us both, the camera on the desk in front of him.

It was a little Kodak disposable, bright orange against the gleaming wooden surface and pristine white blotter.

Travis sat up straight. "What...what...Johnny? Grandpa? What the heck happened?"

Grandpa picked up the camera between two fingers and dropped it back on the desk as if it were something dead. "You violated our trust, Travis...the trust of your family, everyone here at Stanton's Fall, and everyone in the Company, for that matter. That's what happened." He leaned forward, dark eyes glittering in the light of the smoking kerosene lamp. "You were told cameras were forbidden. Weren't you?"

"I'm sorry," he said. His chin had a noticeable dark-blue bruise. "I-I wanted to get photos of everyone...of you and Grandma and Johnny. Wh-what's wrong with that?"

"Nothing," said Grandpa, looking angrier than I ever saw him. He pulled out a piece of paper from his desk drawer. "Except that you and both your parents signed this."

Travis peered at the paper. I didn't have to see it to know that whatever it else it said, it specified that no cameras were to be brought to Stanton's Fall. We didn't need cameras. Several times a year, professional photographers employed by the Company took all the family photos anyone could ask for. We had a longstanding appointment with one tomorrow morning for presents, in fact. There was going to be plenty of photographs.

The back of my head was beginning to throb and when I touched it gingerly, I could feel a knot beginning to rise. I glanced at Travis. I was beginning to hate him, the fucking idiot.

"There's something you need to understand about Stanton's Fall, young man," said Grandpa, and for the first time, ever, he didn't sound like Grandpa. His voice had a hard edge, his eyes reminded me of the train's black gleam. "You step foot over the border of Stanton's Fall, and you step out of the United States of America. This is Company land, and the Company takes care of us. We follow Company rules for the privilege. And one of those rules is no cameras. Do you understand me?"

Travis nodded. He looked scared, and he knew better than to look at me.

But Grandpa wasn't finished. He leaned forward, his massive hands clasped together. "It wasn't my idea to bring you here. I was against it from the beginning, but Iris wanted it. So against my better judgment, I went along with it. But don't you dare step over the line again, boy. You hear me? Don't you dare. Because you step over that line again, and I may not be able to pull you back over it." He paused. "And I know you don't understand me. Let's keep it that way."

We weren't allowed to listen to the Gipper. A car brought us home, with a uniformed driver who opened and shut the doors for us silently.

The house was silent, the Christmas tree lights twinkling in the living room. I didn't feel very Christmas-y. Mom was at the hotel, Grandma and Grandpa was still at the station house, celebrating with the town, enjoying the entertainment and the annual gala. To say I was furious was an understatement. Grandpa hadn't even wanted to hear my side, hadn't even asked me to explain my side of things. I'd been tarred with the same brush as Travis and I was bitterly resentful.

I ignored Travis when I let us in with the key under the mat.

I didn't even say good night when I went upstairs to bed.

IV

I was tired, and I didn't hear Travis follow me, didn't hear my grandparents come home. The next thing I knew, my grandmother was shaking me frantically awake. "Johnny, Johnny. Johnny, wake up."

I was groggy with sleep. The day before had tired me out and I remember how relieved I'd been when my head sank into my pillow that I was about to get a break from Travis for a few hours. He was snoring on the other side of the room. "Grandma?" The room was still dark, but light from the hallway slanted into my eyes. "What's wrong?"

"Your grandpa needs you, down at the station. There's been an accident...he needs your help."

That jolted me wide awake. "Is he...is he okay?"

"Yes, yes, he's fine, but he needs your help. Now get dressed and get down there... I have a basket of sandwiches and a couple thermoses of coffee ready. Dress warm... you're going to need it."

"Sandwiches? Coffee?" I stumbled out of bed. What kind of accident requires sandwiches and coffee? But I did as she said. Careful not to wake Travis, in the moonlight it struck me how much he really did resemble a young Elvis. If only he wasn't such an idiot.

In the kitchen, she gave me a garment that seemed to be some kind of long underwear. "Put this on under your clothes," she said.

"But Grandma, I just got..."

"Do as I say, boy."

The fabric was quilted, thicker than my long johns, and shot through with some sort of metallic thread, that felt, when I pressed on it or bent my elbows and knees, a little like chain mail. It was surprisingly light and not as bulky as I thought it would be. And it was much warmer. And obviously made for a bigger man, because the sleeves and legs were too long.

When I came back out, she was holding out something that looked like a hat, and a backpack from which I could see two thermoses. "Grandpa will show you how to put this on... the gloves are in the bag. So are the sandwiches and a few cookies. You hurry on down there now... you two be careful." Her voice had a little catch that she didn't allow me time to question.

Instead she pushed me out the door. The floodlights snapped on. I had no idea what time it was, but just like in the poem, the town was buttoned up tight. I half jogged, half ran to the Station House.

I found my grandfather hooking up a trailer to the specially modified Jeep he used to patrol the miles and miles of track he was responsible for. "What happened, Grandpa?"

He swore softly under his breath, something that sounded a lot like, "Motherfucking sons of bitches" before he said, "There was a second, smaller train due to tonight... supposed to be here around midnight. Just a few miles out of town, they hit a couple moose."

"Oh, no." Of all the hazards that threatened the trains, moose were no small problem. Unlike most other creatures, moose don't run when something is bearing down on them. And they're huge, or they can be.

"Oh, yeah," said Grandpa. He handed me a shotgun, and more than few rounds. "You remember how to use this?"

"Sure I do." I was beyond confused at that point. The underwear was starting to itch. The equipment in the back of the Jeep was confusing, because it looked like was mostly ammunition and axes, not exactly what I'd pack if I were going to dig out a train. Then he handed a roll of duct tape. "What's this for?"

"I'll explain in the Jeep. Grandma give you the headpiece?"

For a second I didn't understand what he was talking about, and then I reached into my backpack. "You mean, this?" I pulled out the black thing she'd put on top of the sandwiches and cookies.

"That's it. Let's get it attached to the collar, and then just leave it off your head until we get to where we're going. It's too uncomfortable otherwise."

I knew better than to ask. I let him show me how it attached to the high collar, how it snapped into place with industrial grade snaps. When it was on it fitted like a cross between a ski mask and a sock. It had openings for ear pieces that seemed to amplify the sound, not block it. When I asked Grandpa about this, he just nodded and said, "That's right."

We got in the Jeep. Grandpa put it in gear and we were off, the trailer bumping along behind us. With the back seat full, we were obviously not going to get people. So what were we going after?

But I wasn't Travis. I knew I'd be told when I needed to know. The first thing Grandpa said, though, just confused even more. "You know any Elvis songs, son?"

"Elvis?" I wasn't even sure I heard correctly.

"Never mind. It won't matter, I'm sure."

I couldn't help it. "Sure about what, Grandpa?"

He reaches over and pats my knee. "Sure you'll do just fine, Johnny. Just fine."

We rode the rest of the way in silence, the two way radio crackling on occasion with what sounded like the most routine of chatter. I heard snatches of Christmas carols hummed, I heard a few sounds that sounded like metal grinding against metal. I heard a lot of static. But otherwise, except for the fact the night was pitch-black, and the grim expression on my grandfather's face, we could've been out for a late night drive.

We were maybe 10 minutes out of town when we came upon the train wreck. In the eerie light of the smoking wreck, I could see pieces of what were obviously two separate moose. The engine lay on its side, a smoking hulk that I could see was quite a bit smaller than the earlier train. It was only pulling a couple cars, however, and both had careened onto their sides, and now half-tilted against the high snow bank on the far side of the tracks.

There were splashes of blood on the snow, a spray on the window of the engine. The remains of Grandma's clam chowder backed up in my throat.

As if anticipating my reaction, Grandpa said, "Get ready, boy. This won't be pretty." But instead of getting out, he turned to me. "Get that hood on." As I was struggling to align the ear pieces with my ears and to secure the flaps, he handed me something that looked like a modified miner's helmet, with a plastic eye shield, and lights in both the front and back. "Strap this under your chin."

"What's the light in back for, Grandpa?" I asked, struggling to get it securely buckled.

"So nothing can sneak up behind you," he replied. "Now make sure your shotgun's loaded."

The hair went up on the back of my neck, but the habit of obedience was so ingrained I did as I was told.

"Be careful getting out of the car," he said.

Finally survival won out. "What's out there, Grandpa," I blurted. "What're you so afraid of?"

And in that moment, a face, a hideous semblance of a human face, launched itself into my window. It wasn't much more than a skull with shreds of hair adhering in places, rheumy eyes shriveled into sockets so dark I don't believe the thing could see. The rotting leather of its nose twisted sideways as it pressed itself against the glass, jaws gnashing, what looked like the remnants of a metal plate clanking against the window frame.

I screamed.

Grandpa put a hand on my shoulder. "Lock your door, boy."

The thing clawed at the window with its teeth. In the light of my headlamp, I could see its arms were bound in a straitjacket of some kind. It left streaks of what looked fresh blood on the glass. I didn't know who

– or what – it was, but I knew I wasn't going to let it kill me. I raised my own gun, just in case it somehow got my door open.

Grandpa eased his own door open. "Keep it focused on you, boy."

I knocked on the glass with the tip of the gun and the thing redoubled its efforts, just as a single blast exploded its head in a shower of putrid flesh. As it collapsed, Grandpa pushed his way through the snow, and opened my door. "You can come out. Try not to step on that poor son of a bitch."

I opened the door and found that my legs were shaking when I tried to stand on them. The thing collapsed in the snow bore a resemblance to a large puppet, so unnaturally splayed were its limbs. But beneath the strait jacket, it appeared to be wearing a uniform. A military uniform. Against the snow, the Army green and brightly shined shoes stood out like beacons. "Grandpa," I whispered. "Who…what…what is this?"

"That one…that was Glenn Miller. About time that poor son of a bitch bought the farm for good."

"What? Who….?" Before Grandpa could reply, I broke off because the sound that came from the train didn't sound quite human. But it spoke a word… "Help me," in such a low, tortured groan, I knew it had to be.

"Stay here by the car, Johnny. Keep your eyes open. I'll take care of that." Grandpa turned on his heel, marched over to the train. The tortured pleading got louder. My skin crawled. I couldn't help looking down at the thing in the snow. I racked my brain. Glenn Miller, Glenn Miller. The name meant something to me, but I couldn't place it.

I looked up at a sound like shotgun being cocked, in time to see Grandpa aim into the cab of the train and shoot.

The moaning stopped instantly.

"Grandpa!" I couldn't help it. I'd just seen my grandfather shoot what sounded like another human being in cold blood. "Grandpa, what the fuck? What the fuck is going on here?"

He looked up, loaded the gun. "Don't come over here, John. You don't need to see this."

"Grandpa, you need to tell me what we're doing here. What the fuck is this thing… and why'd you just kill that man?"

For a split second, I met my grandfather's eyes and I thought he'd tell me. Instead he said, "I didn't bring you out here to answer questions, Johnny. Now that was the engineer…there's at least three more out there… one crew, two more of those… things." He pointed to the thing at my feet. "Make sure your back light is, and let's go."

The woods are empty, dark and deep. I'd written my last English paper on Robert Frost and I never expected to think of him again, but those words rolled through my mind as Grandpa and I set off through the trees, following what was clearly a trail. The air was so cold it froze the hairs in my nose, but beneath the enormous trees, the snow wasn't that deep.

I'd never been so far in the forest around Stanton's Fall at night, never realized how enormous the trees. Some had to be as big around as any redwood. We pushed further in, and I realized that not only were the trees huge, but that there was no underbrush.

The tracks wove through the trees, in a crazy zigzag that doubled back and around on itself. Suddenly Grandpa put his arm across my chest, halting me in midstep. He sniffed the air, pointed toward a stand of trees, and slowly raised the gun, gesturing for me to do the same.

"Love me tender, love me true," he crooned.

Once more the hair rose on the back of my neck as the special ear pieces picked up a noise, a soft noise I know I wouldn't have otherwise heard, even in the silence of the forest night.

"You're so young and beautiful…. You're everything to me," Grandpa sang, louder.

I trained my gun on the same spot in which he had his, finger poised against the trigger. And from between the trunks of two massive trees, in the harsh light of the headlamps, a shape shambled out, remnants of what had been a straitjacket hanging from its shoulders and what remained of its arms, which were missing below the elbows. Underneath the torn white fabric, I could see a powder blue suit that shimmered.

It raised its arms, heading right for us.   "Are you going to shoot it, Grandpa?" The closer it got the better I could see that it wasn't anywhere near as decayed looking as the first creature. In fact, except for the snarl on its face, I recognized who it was... or had been. "Are you going to shoot Elvis?"

"Not if I can help it." To my complete astonishment, he slung the gun over his shoulder and removed the rope from his hip. With the ease of a cowboy, he lassoed the shambling form.   Elvis lunged at him, jaws snapping, truncated arms waving wildly. Part of his face was smashed in, and I could see part of what had to be his brain leaking out around his ear. Grandpa wrapped the rope around Elvis, and pushed him face down into the snow, well away from the teeth. "Give me the duct tape."

With a few deft turns, he had Elvis's mouth taped up so he was no longer in danger of biting us. We tied his legs together and dragged him through the snow, back to the waiting Jeep. Grandpa opened the trailer and we placed him into it, still writhing.

We shut the trailer. "Come on, boy," said Grandpa. "There's one more out there somewhere."

"One more what, Grandpa? One more zombie?" Travis asked as he stepped around the Jeep.

I just about pissed my special long-johns. "Jesus fucking Christ, Travis," I said, sagging against the side of the trailer. "What the fuck are you doing here?"

Although he was wearing a parka and boots, he didn't have a gun. Or any of our protective gear, which now, that I'd seen what we were out to find, I understood exactly why I needed it. I thought Grandpa would be angry, but he wasn't half as angry as I thought he'd be. He seemed resigned in a grim sort of way that Travis had showed up, almost as if he'd expected it.

"Stay behind me, you damn fool kid," was all he said.

"Can't I have a gun, too?" Travis asked, as we took off in the opposite direction, after another set of tracks.

"Shut up, boy," hissed Grandpa. "Unless you want us killed."

My heart was pounding. It was bad that Travis had showed up, I just had a feeling. It was like in a horror movie, when the cute blonde girl opens the door to the basement, and you know she just shouldn't. And just like in a real horror movie, I had a terrible feeling there was nothing I could do about it.

Because of the ear pieces, Travis's breathing sounded like a freight train in my ears. The snow crunched under our boots, the long white trails of our breath conjured like ghosts. I'd seen Glenn Miller's head reduced to blood-spray and a stump, and the King of Rock n' Roll corralled and thrown in the back of a trailer. "Grandpa," I said, as quietly as I could, when we paused to let Grandpa sniff the air, "any idea who we're looking for?"

He shook his head, shrugged. "Young guy ... last name of Morrison, I think. Another musician... the shareholders love their musicians. Used to be part of a group...the windows, the doors, something like that."

"Morrison?" said Travis. "Jim Morrison? Of the Doors? He's been dead ... since 1971."

"Damn it," cried Grandpa, pushing Travis out of the way of the shambling thing that had suddenly appeared without warning from behind one of the massive tree trunks.

The thing lunged for Travis, who turned, saw what was bearing down on him, and screamed. He leaped at least six feet past me, and took off running, in the direction we'd come from, toward the Jeep, toward the wreck of the train.

Like Elvis, Jim wasn't in much better shape. His strait jacket was in shreds, but his face mask was intact, and unlike the others, we didn't have to worry about him biting us. Not that he didn't try, and not that Grandpa put a few strips of duct tape around his mouth just to be sure.

We put a few strips of duct tape around his ankles and dragged him back to the trailer. Grandpa unlocked the trailer, and we threw him in next to Elvis. Both of them looked a lot worse for wear, but at least we had them.

Travis was cowering in the back seat when we got in the front. "Grandpa? Johnny? What the fuck are those things? Are they really zombies...like in the movies?"

Grandpa shot him a look over his shoulder. I expected him to tell Travis to shut up, but instead he took a deep breath. "Those things, as you call them are not zombies...they're the result of a Company research and development program into something they call ADR – after death rehabilitation. They started it in World War II – the one poor bastard was Glenn Miller. I know neither of you know who he was, but every year the shareholders like trotting him around to the Chattanooga Choo-Choo."

"I know who Glenn Miller was," Travis said slowly. "He had an orchestra... he disappeared over the English Channel in December, 1944."

I glanced over my shoulder at Travis. In the moonlight, he definitely didn't look like Elvis, at least not the Elvis bumping around in the trailer. I felt sick to my stomach and I wanted to go home and take a shower. I don't think I've ever been so glad to see the Station House, nor so disappointed when we drove past it without so much as a tap on the brake.

I glanced at Grandpa. There was no doubt about it. We were heading toward the Compound.

I recognized the gatekeeper right away. He hadn't been at the celebration earlier, because Christmas Eve was one of the busiest nights of his year. But by the time we came rolling up to the stone gatehouse, the road leading further into the compound was totally deserted.

Stan waved us down and Grandpa rolled to a stop beside him. He put the window down and leaned on his elbow. "Merry Christmas, Stan."

"And to you, John... you – ah, you have the –ah, guests of honor intact?"

"I wouldn't call them intact," Grandpa said, with a tap of his fingers on the steering wheel. "But I have them."

"Johnny," said Stan, seeming to recognize me just then, "you out helping your grandpa tonight?"

"Yes, sir," I answered.

"You're a good boy, John," replied Stan.

"And my other grandson," Grandpa said, with a nod to the back seat, where Travis had finally realized he'd be better off being quiet. "In fact, Stan, while I deliver the guests of honor, can I... could I ask you to entertain young Travis here? He's only 16."

"Absolutely," answered Stan, breaking into a broad smile. "The wife's just getting out the Santa cookies... you like marshmallows or whipped cream in your cocoa, young man?"

I thought I heard Travis mumble "Either one," as he stumbled out of the car.

I thought Grandpa and Stan exchanged some sort of a look before he put the car back in gear and we drove off.

"You're a good boy, John," said Grandpa. "Grandma and I... and your mother, of course... we say it all the time... how lucky we are, how proud." He glanced at me out of the corner of his eye and I sat up straighter.

No one went to the Compound before their 18th birthday. What grandpa was doing was breaking a rule...and I'd never seen him even imagine breaking a rule. I didn't think the universe would hold together if Grandpa broke a rule.

But break it he did, driving directly up to what looked like a very large log cabin. As the lights of our Jeep illuminated the front door, it opened and a short, older man came outside to greet us. It was the Overseer, himself. He was wearing a red velvet bathrobe with the Company insignia on the breast pocket, and what looked like white pajamas under it.

I glanced at Grandpa nervously. From the corner of my eye, I saw a team of the black-uniformed Squad, the people who handle the clean-ups, from snow removal to garbage, march out from a very long low building that resembled either a stable or a garage. As the Overseer opened my door, they swarmed over the trailer, detaching it from the back of the Jeep, and somehow removing it all together by the time I managed to put my feet outside the car.

"Merry Christmas, Johnny," the Overseer said, with a smile like Santa. "We missed you tonight, downtown."

"Sir, I…uh…"

"It was my decision to involve my Johnny, sir," Grandpa said, before I could manage anything more coherent than a few mumbles. "When the accident happened… he was young, strong… and he's eighteen next month."

"Of course he is." The Overseer clapped Grandpa on the shoulder. "We're just grateful for your fast action, John…even if…" He sighed and shook his head. "Even if…well, we'll see what can be done."

Grandpa took a deep breath. "You'll see for yourself, sir…I'm not sure the guests of honor are… capable of joining in this year."

The Overseer smiled, beneficent and bubbly as a cherry soda. "Not to worry, John… in fact, would you mind coming with me? I know it's late and you want to get back to your lovely wife." He winked at me. "Visions of sugarplums dancing in your head, young man, I'll be bound. I remember what it was to be 17." He smiled, broadly, as genuine an elf as any Santa. "But there's someone who wants to shake your hand. He's very interested in our ADR program."

He was interrupted by a uniformed servant, whispering in his ear. "Ah, of course. The festivities are continuing… please, will you walk with me?"

We were hardly dressed to go inside the mansion, but the direction the Overseer gestured was up a path that led away from the house, from the garages, if that's what they were, and toward the curve of the rail-road track glimmering under the moonlight.

The entire Compound was set upon a rise, so that gradually, the path rose uphill, toward another series of buildings, behind which rose a flickering orange glow. It lit the night sky so brightly it blotted out the stars.

The building we entered resembled a gym. I found myself on a long catwalk, above what appeared to be a swimming pool empty of water.

But it was full, of the swarming, naked bodies of maybe a hundred or so kids, all somewhere between the ages of maybe ten or twelve and my age.

White uniformed attendants were using long fire hoses to squirting them down with some sort of oily, viscous substance that clung to them in white slimy gobs. From the sidelines, they shouted down to the kids: "Bend over... spread those cheeks... pull it through your hair."

One noticed the Overseer standing on the catwalk and gave a thumbs up. "Right on schedule, sir."

"Excellent!" replied the Overseer. He leaned over, pointed down into the pit of naked kids. "Save those two little chocolates for me, will you, Bob?"

"You've got them, sir! Hey, Marv...those two in the corner?"

As I watched with a stupefied horror, two attendants hoisted a dark-skinned boy and girl of about Travis's age, with towels because their bodies were so slippery with whatever it was they were coated with.

My grandfather tapped me on the arm, pushed me so that my back was turned to what was happening below and behind.

"Look who's here," said the Overseer.

I've yet to understand why so many American Presidents adopt cowboy gear, but in the Gipper's case, he wore his with swagger and a certain panache. "I just wanted to congratulate you, Mr. Stanton," he was saying to Grandpa, as he shook his hand vigorously with both of his. "You did a heck of a job tonight, all alone, in the dark and the cold. That was real bravery and I want you to know I, on behalf of Americans everywhere, appreciate your efforts."

"I wasn't actually alone, Mr. President," my grandfather replied. "I couldn't have done it alone... my grandson, Johnny, he helped."

"This fine young man?" The Gipper shook my hand so hard I thought my arm might come off.

I had to drag my attention away from what was going on below. The air was filled with a peculiar smell, astringent, almost that re-minded me of my grandmother's sheets. I sniffed, tentatively, trying to place it.

"Like that?" said the Overseer, leaning in conspiratorially. "That's lavender, imported from the South of France. I just love the smell of lavender, don't you?" He took a deep breath and shut his eyes, as doors opened at one end of the enormous pool, and more attendants emerged to encourage the kids to pass through.

"What's that stuff," I blurted.

"Emollient," he replied, smiling blandly. "Makes them nice and cr-" He caught my grandfather's eye. "Slippery."

"We'd best be getting back," my grandfather said.

"Absolutely," said Reagan. "I'm going back to the party... you know the owner is due to arrive any minute?"

"I'll be there," said the Overseer. The door behind us opened and a cold blast hit my face. I took a deep breath and stepped outside, grateful to be out.

The overseer's word was echoing in my mind. Slippery. It makes them slippery. Slippery... or crispy?

Wasn't that what he'd been about to say?

No, my mind rejected that. I turned back to my grandfather and the overseer, standing on the stoop, shaking hands. Maybe, I thought, this was all just some strange dream.

We walked back alone, toward the Jeep. "Grandpa," I began.

"You'll know soon enough, boy," he said.

Our breath steamed in front of us, the silence rose. My grandfather's footsteps quickened. "Come on, boy. Let's get you home."

At the gatehouse, Stan flagged us down. "Catch a ride back to town with you, John? Everyone else is gone...and I don't like to be here when..."

"No one does," answered my grandfather.

"Where's Travis?" I asked, looking around.

"Oh," said the gatekeeper, "He's down for the night."

My grandmother had hot chocolate and marshmallows waiting, but I couldn't drink it. For some reason, the melting marshmallows reminded me of the sticky gobs of stuff on all those kids. All those kids, I thought. Every time I thought about all those kids, about what was going to happen to them, my stomach twisted.

I pushed my mug away, and my grandfather slammed a shot glass, full to the brim, in front of me, ignoring my grandmother's squawk. "Take it, Johnny. Sometimes a man needs something stronger than chocolate." He looked over his shoulder at Grandma. "The Overseer spoke to Johnny personally."

"He did?" Grandma smiled, her face growing soft with pride.

"Seemed to like him…I was proud." He clapped his hand on my back. "You did me proud out there, tonight, Johnny. I know you saw some things you weren't expecting –or even prepared- to see, but you did well. You did great."

Despite the visions of the kids, of the stuff, of the orange glow in the sky, I felt myself swell with the praise. My grandfather was hardly ever so effusive. My grandmother gave me a hug and a kiss on the cheek. "You sleep in as late as you please, Johnny. It won't be Christmas until you get up."

V

Maybe it was the whiskey, maybe it was exhaustion, but I slept like a really dead dead man until I heard the crunch of a big black Company car in the driveway. I lifted my head off the pillow in time to see a limousine pull up and let someone in a Boston Red Sox hat get out. Travis, I thought. I put my robe and slippers on… it was my Christmas after all, and went downstairs expecting to see my cousin and my grandparents.

But instead of my cousin, my uncle Cole was standing just inside the front door, my mother, grandparents, Nick Cabot, the Town Manager, and the Overseer seated at the dining room table.

"I want my son," Cole said. "I'm here for my son and I won't leave without him."

"Sit down, Cole," said the Overseer. "It's good to see you again after all this time, even if it looks as if you've had something of a rough time of it lately." He nods at my uncle's unshaven face, disheveled clothes.

"You fucking demon." Cole drew himself up. "I'm putting food on my family's table, making an honest living... I guess that wouldn't be something you'd know anything about."

I halted on the second step, stunned, wondering if I should just turn on my heel and run back to bed, before any of the adults appeared to notice me. I thought about the kids in the pit. No, I thought immediately. No, surely not. Grandpa, Grandma... no one would let anything as terrible as what I was imagining happen to Travis. Surely not.

"Come on and join us, Johnny," called the Overseer. "You were there last night... come have a seat and tell your Uncle Cole exactly what happened last night. With your cousin, that is."

I sidled down the steps, hands in my pockets, feeling as guilty as a nine year old caught raiding the cookie jar.

"You're not in trouble, John," said Nick Cabot.

"Just tell Uncle Cole the truth," said my mother.

"The honest truth," said the Overseer. "Iris, darling, would you get the young man a cup of coffee? A strong cup, by the looks of him. And one for Cole, too...give him something to pour his whiskey in, right, Cole?"

I sank into a chair. "Travis got in trouble last night...he brought a camera to the Station House for Christmas Eve. We got sent home and then... last night... when Grandpa got called out... uh, Grandma woke me up. I got dressed...I thought Travis was asleep."

"So did I," said my grandmother. She put a mug of steaming coffee in front of me, and waved the pot around. "Freshen up, anyone?"

"No one's blaming you, Iris, dear," said the Overseer with a flash of white teeth.

My grandmother put a mug down at the seat opposite my mother. "Come on, Cole, we're going to talk this out like civilized adults."

"Talk it out? What the fuck are you thinking? You've let them kidnap my kid on some trumped up excuse, and you expect me to talk it out?"

"We realize you're upset, Cole, but you do understand a kidnapping charge would never hold up in court?"

"That's because you own every judge from the First Circuit on down."

"I'm glad we understand each other, Cole," replied the Overseer. "Why not let Johnny finish his story, unless he'd like some toast first? The sourdough is excellent, I'm going to have to steal a loaf for the owner."

I took a quick sip of coffee, but set the mug down quickly. "I thought Travis was asleep. I... I went down to the Station House like Grandma said, and I... met up with Grandpa... and um... we... took the Jeep out to the wreck.   And in the middle of the, uh... clean-up.... Travis surprised us."

At that my uncle made a little sound that could've been a moan. His face drained of color behind his scruff of beard.

"Sit down, Cole," said the Overseer firmly, and he did.

My mother pushed the sugar bowl toward him. "You still take two?"

"I'll take my fucking son," he screamed, slamming his fist on the table. "Now!"

"Cole, I have the contract here," the Overseer said, removing a thick white envelope. "You signed it, his mother signed it, and Travis signed it. So let's hear Johnny out, shall we, before we weigh our options?"

"There's only one acceptable option," Cole snarled.

"Shut up, Cole, you always were a fool," said my grandfather. "There's always lots of options... when you deal with the Company, that is."

The Overseer smiled. "John Stanton, you are indeed a company man."

Cole put his elbows on the table, and his face in his hands. "My God," he whispered, and it sounded like a real prayer. "Lots of options? Oh, yeah, the Company gives you options...sure, like at a casino, where the house inevitably wins. But they give you lots of options as to how to lose."

"And you might be a fool," laughed the Overseer, "But you always did have a way with words. So, Johnny, whenever you're ready?"

I looked from my mother to my grandfather. My grandfather's face was like chiseled stone, my mother smiled reassuringly. "Johnny, you're not in any kind of trouble at all...in fact, we're all very proud of you. So just go on, don't worry. Travis got himself in trouble."

"We... uh... we found Elvis... I mean, Mr. Presley...and we put him in the trailer, so he couldn't get any more banged up, and were trying to figure out which direction the third one had gone –"

"There's a third one now?" Cole stared at the Overseer.

The Overseer shrugged. "That's not my department. Go on, Johnny."

"So we were looking for tracks, and Travis just... just showed up. He almost got himself shot. We let him tag along, until we found the third, and then he got so scared he ran all the way back to the Jeep. We captured Mr. Morrison, put him in the Jeep with Mr. Presley, cleaned up what we could of Mr. Miller, and brought them all to you, sir." I nodded at the Overseer. "We left Travis at the gate house, drinking cocoa. With marshmallows."

Cole ignored me. He looked the Overseer with the most unmitigated hatred I've ever seen in any human being's expression, except, perhaps, my own. He spoke directly to him, as if they were the only two people in the room. And in a way they were, because they were the only two who mattered. "I know what you do up there on Christmas Eve." He spoke through gritted teeth. "Tell me... tell me that didn't happen to my son."

"Of course not," exclaimed the Overseer. "My God, Cole...the things you imagine. Have you examined the depths of your own dark soul recently? It's quite a violent place, isn't it? No wonder you drink."

"Give me Travis and let us go, and I - we - will never contact any of these people again."

"You'd do that to your family, Cole?" said the Overseer, very quietly, so quietly I suddenly turned colder than I was last night in the woods. He took a deep breath, leaned forward, his expression kind, almost, definitely concerned. "You see, the thing is... I'm afraid we can't let you have Travis – he violated just about every condition, every clause; he did everything he was told expressly more times than once not to do. Am I right?" He looked around the table at the rest of us.

And I nodded, because everyone else did, even though I had no idea with what I was really agreeing.

"Everything he agreed not to do, everything you agreed he wouldn't do, everything his mother agreed he wouldn't do...Cole, do you see where I'm going here?"

"What do you intend to do with him?" Cole's eyes were empty, his face even more haggard.

"Nothing more than what might've happened anyway, if you'd stayed, and kept your proper place. He's ours, now, Cole, that's all, and we'll make him a Company man. A Company man like your father, like your nephew. Like me." The Overseer smiled. "And what's so bad about that?" He looked around the high-ceilinged dining room, the massive sideboard, the portrait of the first John Stanton, the one for whom the town was named, smiling down from above the mantel.

"I want to see him, explain to him...tell him..."

The Overseer signed. "I'm afraid you both forfeited that right..." he leafed through the pages of the contract. "Yes, right here, you see? Clause three?"

With a curse, Cole lunged across the table, arms extended, reaching for the Overseer. And in one motion, my grandfather rose, grabbed his son by the neck and twisted it, with a loud snap.

Cole slumped like a chicken to the dining room floor.

"Indeed, John Stanton," said the Overseer, in the silence that followed the heavy thump. "You are a Company man."

Grandpa retired the summer after I graduated from high school. I stepped into his shoes after a three month tour of Europe, courtesy of the Company, of course.

I'm the youngest Station Master in Company history, but Grandpa had the job for nearly twice as long as anyone else. A couple of the shareholders showed up for my induction, and even the Owner sent a commendation. Whatever shame, whatever cloud, hung over the family in the wake of my uncle's actions, was totally and completely absolved by my grandfather's.

As it turned out, what goes on at the Compound isn't anywhere near as bad as what I was imagining. Bad, maybe, but not that bad.

And, as I suspected, both Elvis and Jim were too torn up in the accident to be of much use to anyone, even as the living dead, any more. I don't know where they found the new Jim Morrison, but Travis does indeed make a damn fine Elvis.

The End

OTHER TITLES:

SF/Fantasy:
Daughter of Prophecy
Children of Enchantment
The Misbegotten King
The Knight, the Harp & the Maiden
Silver's Edge
Silver's Bane
Silver's Lure

Romance:
A Once & Future Love
The Ghost & Katie Coyle
Love's Labyrinth
The Highwayman
Wickham's Folly
Wickham's Fancy

High Interest/Low Level:
How David Met Sarah
When David was Surprised

About the Author

———

Born and raised at the South Jersey shore, Anne Kelleher wrote her first novel in high school. She now divides her time between the Big Island of Hawaii, and the northwest hills of Connecticut. An incurable optimist, Annie refuses to succumb to dystopic visions of a bleak future, and insists that the world we can create is only as limited as our imaginations.

Find more of Annie's work on Amazon, and connect with Annie on Facebook at www.facebook.com/annekelleherauthor, on Twitter at @annekelleherauthor, or at www.annekelleher.net.

www.ingramcontent.com/pod-product-compliance
Lightning Source LLC
Chambersburg PA
CBHW021046130626
46552CB00005B/2045